Cheerleading Can Be Murder

Horror High Series: Book One

By Carissa Ann Lynch

Cheerleading Can Be Murder

First Print Edition: April 2016

LIMITLESS PUBLISHING

Limitless Publishing, LLC
Kailua, HI 96734
www.limitlesspublishing.com

Formatting: Limitless Publishing

ISBN-13: 978-1-68058-559-9
ISBN-10: 1-68058-559-2

Dedication

Dedicated to: Violet, Dexter, Tristian, and Shannon. You guys are the best cheerleaders a girl could ask for.

Prologue

The Sociopath

Do you want to know what death smells like? What it *really* smells like?

Take a pound of raw meat—I recommend ground chuck. Stick it in a vacuum-sealed container. Place the container in the fridge and leave it there. A few months later, take it out. Remove the lid.

Nothing can prepare you for the brick wall that smacks your face, filling every orifice of your body simultaneously.

That smell…not only will it blow you away, but smells like that, they stick with you.

Lifeless meat in a tight, confined space produces a smell sharp enough to burn the lashes off your eyelids.

So, for the rest of the day you'll be moving along…and then some small thing reminds you—little Tommy's Happy Meal or a dump truck rolling by on garbage day—and your nose twitches, remembers, and the hairs inside your nostrils stiffen. Your throat tickles in the back, bile rising, and your belly rolls uncomfortably. You try to push the thought aside, to forget that smell, but…you can't.

Like I said, smells stick with you. Even months—maybe years—later, you'll be walking along, minding your own business, when something—anything, really—reminds you of that smell.

I know what death smells like…

The house is empty, silent. The quiet consumes me, a welcoming blanket…a sign that it's finally time.

The mini-fridge was my grandma's idea. A teenager now, she thought I deserved my own little space for drinks and snacks.

I squatted down in front of it, listening to its hum. My heart pumped, excitement building. Today was the day.

It'd been nearly six months now since I started my little "experiment." I'd kept a journal, taking notes on my observations regarding the specimen. A disciplined endeavor.

I'd done a lot of monitoring, but today was the day to *really* observe, up close and personal.

I opened the fridge, enjoying the sticky "smooch" sound of the rubber seals on each side separating. A couple cans of soda sat on the top shelf. Generic cola, probably expired. On the bottom was my Tupperware container, its red cap securely fastened in place. Keeping all the smells inside…

Carefully, I slid the container off the shelf, carrying it to the center of my bedroom floor, tiptoeing like a gymnast on a balance beam. I plopped on my belly, burning my bare knees across the carpet. I pressed my face to the plastic, looking inside like it was a tiny window. I made a funny face, pressing my lips to the side and blowing, exposing my teeth.

Two eyes, wide and frozenly frightened, stared back at me through the plastic container. The eyeballs mushy now, there were tiny bits and pieces of egg-white eyeball chunks floating in the fluids surrounding its face. The once shiny black coat faded now to a murky brown color.

Excitedly, I lifted the lid. Taking in the smells of death.

"Meow." I grinned at my stinky friend.

It was a smell I'd never forget…hopefully.

Chapter One

Dakota

In exactly six minutes, the morning bell at Harrow High will ring, inducting me in as a new freshman. Considering it was my first year of high school, I should have been excited about so many things, like hot senior boys, invitations to unchaperoned parties, and getting my driver's license in the spring. Alternatively, I should have been worried about mean older girls, finding my classes, and remembering my locker combination. But there was one thing, and one thing only, that I was excited and worried about—Harrow High's varsity cheerleading tryouts.

I cheered in elementary and middle school, but what I'm talking about now is the Big Leagues. Harrow's varsity cheerleading squad was one of the best in the nation for cheerleading competitions, and the basketball team they represented on game nights wasn't too shabby either. I wanted it so bad I could taste it, and I'd been preparing for this my whole life with dance lessons and intense gymnastics training. I was skilled and peppy enough to deserve a spot on the team, but it simply wasn't that easy. There were so many factors standing in my way of getting a fair shot at my dream.

Here's the deal—only six girls could make it, and for the past few years, the same six girls had held tightly to their positions. This year was different though because two of the six had graduated, leaving two vacant spots. Everyone who tried out was supposed to have an equal advantage, including the four returning cheerleaders, but I had no doubt that those same four would get their spots back.

The first of the four returning members was Tasha Faraday, a lovely senior with dirty blonde hair, killer legs, and double D breasts despite being perfectly petite. Looks aside, she was a brilliant tumbler, the designated flyer for all pyramids and stunts, and an all-around terrific cheerleader. Her attitude and personality? Well, let's just say those qualities paled in comparison to her cheerleading abilities and attractiveness.

Tasha's two sidekicks, Tally Johannsen and Teresa Darling, made up spots two and three. They were great cheerleaders too, but nobody could steal Tasha's spotlight, not even her two blonde co-stars. Everyone at Harrow High referred to Tasha, Tally, and Teresa as the Triple Ts. In middle school, they were legends. Now it's my chance to join them.

The fourth returning cheerleader was Monika Rutherford. She was friendlier than the other three, but far less popular. With her olive skin and astounding height of six feet, she stood out like a sore thumb next to the three blondes. She served as a perfect spotter in the back of the pyramid because of her general size and strength.

If all four got spots on the team, then that only left two empty spots to be filled. Normally, I would have been optimistic about my chances of getting one of those spots, but again, there were factors making it nearly impossible. There was a junior girl named Ashleigh Westerfield, who'd been trying out for the squad every year since she was a freshman. This was the first year she actually had a shot of making it, and according to rumors, the coach was going to give her a sympathy vote and let her join the squad.

That left the one open spot. It should be mine, right? Wrong. Brittani Barlow, the bitch of the century and Principal Barlow's daughter, was a freshman this year too, and she was trying out for the squad. Regardless of what anyone else thought, I knew that politics *did* matter, and there was no way the coach was going to turn down the principal's daughter.

So, if the returning four got their spots back, Ashleigh got a sympathy vote, and Brittani took a spot because of her mother, then that left a total of zero spots for me. It was a sad reality and I should have been bummed, but I wouldn't go down without a fight.

I was hoping that, by some miracle, I could beat out the returning four, Ashleigh, or Brittani. And as though my odds of beating out the veterans weren't bad enough, I also had to contend with several other freshmen girls who were going to show up for tryouts today. There was my best friend, Sydney Hargreaves, and my arch nemesis, Genevieve McDermott. And last, but not least, Genevieve's catty best friend, Mariella Martin.

Stepping down from the bus, I smoothed my skirt nervously, approaching a swarm of buzzing new freshman. Boys and girls were gathered in the courtyard of Harrow High, primly pressed and dressed to the nines. The building itself was a gray, one-story, flat-roofed rectangle that sat smack dab in the middle of town. Nothing special, really. But inside that boring blob of a building lay the key to my hopes and dreams, and even if it was childish, I secretly walked with my fingers crossed. My odds of making the team were slim to none, but I couldn't help feeling a teeny tiny glimmer of hope.

The nervous ball of anxiety in the pit of my belly made it look elephantine. Who knew high school would be this intimidating?

Taking a deep breath, I made a beeline for the front door, keeping my head down low, with one foot in front of the other.

"What's up, Dakota?" a boy named Ricki shouted. I wasn't popular—not by any means. But when you grow up in a town this small, everybody knows your name.

"Hi." I smiled at him and a few other girls I recognized.

I pushed my way through the heavy glass doors and began the short hike to my first period of the day, Biology.

Brrrrrrring! There's the bell! *Showtime!*

I dove into a seat in the back, tossing my backpack under the chair. Although I tried to focus on the genial-looking, middle-aged teacher leaning against the desk up front, my gaze was already darting back and forth, eager to pinpoint a clock on the wall. Tryouts seemed so far away…

Class had just begun, but the clock's ticking heartbeat punched the air, resonating in my head rhythmically. *Tick tock*, it mocked me.

Chapter Two

After Biology, I had to endure two more boring classes—Pre-Algebra and American History. In all three of my classes thus far, there hadn't been a single friend or close acquaintance, which really sucked. Even though my mind was fixated on cheerleading tryouts, I'd still been hoping for an interesting first day.

It was time for lunch, and after that I had three more periods—Spanish, Phys Ed, and Study Hall. For now, I focused on finding the lunch room and my best friend, Sydney. As I trudged through flocks of freshmen and upperclassmen, I kept on the lookout for her. It didn't take long to find her.

Sydney was beautiful in her own right, with long, coal-black hair that hung to her waist, flawless skin, and crystal blue eyes. Even though we'd been best friends since grade school, her beauty still stunned me every time I saw her. She reminded me of one of those porcelain dolls that were lovely and creepy at the same time.

When it came to cheerleading, Sydney was less

practiced in dance and tumbling than me, but she learned routines easily and could win people over with her elegance and friendly disposition. The last thing I wanted to do was think of her as competition today but ultimately, that's exactly what she was. I just hoped like hell we could both find some miraculous way to make the squad together…

The thought of the two of us standing next to each other on the sidelines of Harrow's basketball court was enough to make my heart fill with glee.

Sydney was standing in the hallway in front of the lunchroom, looking around anxiously. Searching for me, I presumed. I struggled to push through a wall of seniors to reach her, finally catching her eye. She waved and smiled just as I felt a hard shove from behind. I plunged headlong, struggling to retain my balance, my new Keds skidding noisily across the linoleum floor.

"Watch it, bitch!" came a nasally voice, and I instantly knew it was one of the Triple Ts, specifically the head T—Tasha. I recovered from the push and adjusted my bag, trying to ignore the flush of embarrassment dotting my cheeks.

In middle school, I'd attended a few of the high school games so I knew what Tasha looked like. Unbelievably, she looked even prettier up close. She stood in front of me now, hands on her hips haughtily, with her clan standing as back up behind her. I wasn't in the mood for this. I pushed her back with my shoulder, moving forward through the hallway.

"See you at tryouts today," I shouted over my shoulder, and I couldn't believe the words as they were coming out of my mouth. Challenging Tasha Faraday was a mistake—anyone with half a brain knew that. She pretty much ruled the school. Tasha chuckled behind me, its echo following me down the hallway.

"Don't waste your time, sweetheart. You don't have a chance in hell of making the squad. Right?" she said, riling up her surrounding comrades. I glanced back, recognizing T2 and T3, Tally and Teresa. I also noticed Monika standing behind them in the shadows. Tally and Teresa giggled at Tasha's insult, but Monika glanced down at her shoes apologetically.

By the time I reached Sydney, my blood was still boiling from the confrontation. Sydney was wearing a horrified expression on her face. "You didn't," she hissed, her voice barely above a whisper.

"Oh, screw Tasha. She doesn't scare me." I stuck out my chin defiantly. I reminded myself to keep my head up as we headed to the end of the lunch line.

Sydney told me about her first three classes as we waited in line, trays in hand. I wasn't very hungry, and honestly, I was barely listening to her. All I could think about were Tasha's words, and how I had to somehow prove the Triple Ts wrong.

"Dakota, are you even listening?" Sydney nudged my shoulder playfully.

"I'm sorry. I just have a lot on my mind," I admitted guiltily.

"Tryouts." She nodded sympathetically. "I'm worried about them too."

Sydney probably was nervous for tryouts, but I

suspected that her worries came nowhere near mine. I couldn't seem to think of anything else.

"There he is," Sydney mumbled, rolling her eyes. I didn't have to look. I already knew who she meant. It was Ronnie Becklar, my one-time boyfriend and the biggest heartbreaker of all time. He entered the lunchroom with a strut, dressed in skinny black jeans and a stupid faded t-shirt. He didn't give me a passing glance, but that was no real surprise.

Ronnie and I started dating in eighth grade. I should have known it was too good to be true because he was so popular, and I was so…well, *un*popular. It started with him passing flirty notes in math class. He told me I was pretty and asked for my phone number. Even after we officially became boyfriend and girlfriend, I quickly realized that he liked to flirt with all of the girls, not just me. Toward the end of the school year, he became more distant.

At first, he claimed he was breaking up with me because he wanted to focus on basketball. He'd excelled at sports in middle school, and just like with me and cheerleading, this was his time to shine as a varsity player at Harrow High. But ever since he told me we were breaking up, he'd pretty much acted like I didn't exist.

Ronnie crossed the lunchroom cheerfully, and as I followed his path, my stomach dropped. He took a seat next to his new girlfriend, who also happened to be my arch nemesis, Genevieve McDermott. Genevieve would be at tryouts today too, and I wanted to beat her out for a spot on the team for personal reasons, obviously. Namely, because although Ronnie claimed that he dumped me because he needed to focus on sports, I knew the real reason—he dumped me for Genevieve.

Genevieve was a freshman like me, and we'd been cheering together and competing against each other since the first grade talent show. She had bleached blonde hair, cut in a totally cute and trendy bob. Let's face it—with that hair, she'd look perfect standing next to the Triple Ts on the sidelines. She also had a perfectly sized chest, pearly white teeth, and flirtatious green eyes surrounded by the longest lashes I'd ever seen. She had a reputation for stealing other girls' boyfriends, and I knew she would soon grow tired of Ronnie, moving on to her next victim. Somehow, that thought was comforting.

Genevieve was cozied up at her table with Ronnie and her bestie, Mariella. Mariella was a buxom redhead with long, flowing curls and a freckly, pert nose that actually made her look sweet. That was until she opened her loud, gossiping mouth. Genevieve was busy fawning over Ronnie but Mariella, being the bitchy sidekick that she always was, glared right at me. She flashed a triumphant smile, obviously happy to see her best friend getting one over on me.

"I can't wait to wipe that smile off her face. Off all their faces…" I grumbled to Sydney through clenched teeth.

We found an open spot at a nearby table and plopped down our trays. Sitting down, I caught a glimpse at an overhead clock. *Tick tock.* It was almost twelve-thirty. Only two and a half hours to go until tryouts. *We'll see who Ronnie wants to be with when I get a spot on the team and Genevieve doesn't*, I thought, prying open my milk carton angrily.

I looked around the lunchroom at the rest of my peers, tuning Sydney out, and that was when I saw Ashleigh, the junior whose year it was to finally make the squad. She was perched at a table filled with people, but she was basically sitting alone. No one was talking or looking at her. With hair the color of dirty dishwater, gunmetal-gray eyes, and homely, holey clothing, the first word that came to mind was *lonely*. Under the table, the laces to her ragged running shoes were untied. I couldn't help feeling sorry for her.

In truth, Ashleigh deserved a spot on the team this year. I still had plenty of years ahead of me to make the team when the veterans were gone, but she was getting close to being out of chances. Although I wanted to make the team, I wanted her to make it too, I realized surprisingly.

We can't all make it though, I reminded myself, stuffing a french fry into my mouth. I chewed on it thoughtfully. Two tables up from Ashleigh was Brittani, the principal's daughter. She'd never cheered before, but for some reason, she thought she could just walk into tryouts and claim a spot on the team, simply because her mom was Principal Barlow. That just didn't seem fair, if you asked me.

Brittani was surrounded by her usual entourage of friends, which was a combination of preps and nerds, chatting excitedly, talking about tryouts, no doubt. She was wearing her subtle brown hair in a tight, high ponytail, with a pair of glasses hanging on a string around her neck. Brittani did everything well. She made straight As, played tennis, and even co-coached volleyball on the weekends. *How would she even have time to cheer?* I wondered bitterly.

I stuck more fries and ketchup in my mouth, glaring at Brittani. I had a feeling that, like everything else, Brittani would excel at cheerleading too.

"You're eating those fries like they pissed you off or something," a voice called out from my left. Sydney was beside me, but the voice didn't come from her. I looked over to see my new neighbor, Amanda Loxx, grinning down at me goofily. She took a seat on my right, clinking her tray against mine.

I lived in one of those luxurious, mass-produced McMansions, in the middle of a suburbia called Harrow Hill—hence, the name of my high school. I'd lived here my entire life with my mother, father, and now new baby brother, Vincent. Despite the dozens of similar houses stacked around us, there were always few kids in my age group nearby. The kids in our neighborhood were either too old to want to play with me, or too young for me to do the same.

That all changed when Amanda moved in next door with her grandmother, the infamous Mimi Loxx. Rumor has it, Grandma Mimi used to be a Vegas showgirl, and supposedly, a fast-paced life filled with glamour, drugs, and mini-stardom drove her a little batty. The woman was nearly ninety by now and known around town as a recluse. Local boys delivered her groceries and a professional lawn care service took care of the grounds upkeep. Never outside, the townsfolk of Harrow Hill never heard a peep out of her. That was, until her wild granddaughter Amanda showed up this summer.

Amanda was only fifteen like me, but she didn't look or act like anyone from around here. She had one of those short, Miley Cyrus hairdos, and a silver barbell in her left eyebrow. The first time I met her she was puffing on a Cambridge cigarette in the grassy area at the side of her Grandma Mimi's house, squatting down low next to the air conditioning unit secretively. She had on a black, holey t-shirt with the words ***'Kill Your TV'*** scrawled across it, which I still didn't understand the meaning of.

Even though no one told me directly, I'd overheard the adults—namely, my own parents—talking about how Amanda's father died violently and her mother was an addict. Her parental situation must have been bad if her most lucrative alternative was staying with her eccentric Grandma Mimi.

We didn't have much in common but somehow, we hit it off right from the start. She introduced me to some new styles of music and I helped her paint her nails for the first time. She even let me try some peach schnapps, which was my first drink of alcohol, although I'd never tell her that. We rode bikes, took walks, and talked about boys all summer long. Honestly, it was one of the best summers of my life. Amanda was witty, confident, and all around fun, and I was glad to have her at Harrow

High with me this year.

"Sydney, this is Amanda Loxx, my new neighbor. Amanda, this is the best friend I always talk about, Sydney Hargreaves." They smiled and nodded at each other, but I could sense a small aura of jealousy emanating from both of them. I scooted over on the bench seat, making more room for Amanda.

Several classmates were looking our way, undoubtedly checking out the new girl. I wasn't surprised to see Genevieve and Mariella glaring at us too, but I was a little caught off guard by the furious expression on Genevieve's face as she mean mugged Amanda. I was used to them hating me, but I wasn't quite sure what their vendetta was against Amanda. It didn't take long to figure it out.

"I thought I was her only enemy. Guess I was wrong." I smiled sheepishly at my new neighbor and friend. "Why is she looking at you like that?"

Genevieve narrowed her eyes and pursed her lips evilly, burning holes into Amanda with her liquid-green eyes.

Amanda shrugged. "Oh yeah, *that.* Well, you know how I wasn't on the bus this morning?" I was used to riding the bus alone in the mornings, so I'd completely forgotten all about not seeing her at the bus stop. I nodded.

"Grandma Mimi sleeps 'til noon every day and I forgot to set an alarm. So, I overslept," she explained, shrugging some more. "I decided to walk because…well, everyone knows that Grandma Mimi doesn't leave the house, and she sure as shit doesn't drive."

"You *walked* all the way to school this morning?" I asked incredulously. We were only six miles from Harrow High, but that was quite a long commute traveling by foot.

"That's the thing…I didn't have to walk. Some older boy picked me up a few blocks from our street. He was super cute and nice, and when he pulled up to drop me off, I rewarded him with a kiss on the cheek," Amanda admitted, blushing slightly at the memory of it.

"Yeah, so? What does that have to do with Genevieve? Get to the point," Sydney demanded. I shot Sydney a hateful look. "Sorry," Sydney murmured under her breath.

"It turns out his girlfriend was waiting out front for him, and she saw that he'd given me a lift, and…she also saw the kiss," Amanda explained. "How was I supposed to know he had a girlfriend?"

I knew where this conversation was headed. "Let me guess. The guy you kissed…it was Genevieve's boyfriend, Ronnie, right?" I asked, flatly.

"Yeah, Ronnie. That's his name!" Amanda exclaimed, cheerfully dipping her spoon into a small pudding cup. She filled her mouth with chocolate, then flashed me a silly black-toothed smile.

I rolled my eyes. Yesterday I liked her…ten *minutes* ago, I liked her. But at the moment? Not so much.

Sydney shot me a knowing glance. The last thing I needed was another girl flirting with Ronnie, the crusher of my heart and asshole of the century.

"Oh yeah, I almost forgot!" Amanda chimed in,

interrupting my hateful thoughts. With her painted black nails—the nails *I* painted for her when I still liked her—she slid a pink and purple flier across the table. I stared at it.

"Do you know that cheerleading tryouts are today? I think I'll try out!" Amanda announced gleefully.

I tried my best to stifle a groan, but the sound escaped anyway. I laid my head on the Formica lunch table, reminding myself to breathe. Not only was Amanda after my ex, but now she was taking my spot on the squad?

My first day as a high school freshman was getting off to a rocky start.

Chapter Three

The Sociopath

I closed the door to the bathroom stall behind me. Listened. I didn't hear anyone coming.

My backpack was heavy. Easing it off my shoulders, I rested the bulky thing on the stained toilet seat. I unzipped the pack. Stopped to listen again, but heard no one.

I stuck my hand in the bag, slipping past the new folders and notebooks. The tips of my fingers grazed cool metal.

I gripped the gun in my hand.

I pulled it out, admiring its shiny, sleek design and lightness despite its power.

I moved the backpack from the toilet seat to the floor, taking a seat myself. I pointed the gun at the stall door. From where I sat, there was very little distance between me and the door.

Just enough to extend my arm. I brought my other hand over, using it to steady my grip.

"Bang bang." I aimed the gun at the letter **"S"** in

a crude, **"School sucks"** message written on the door.

Suddenly, the main door to the bathroom swung open, loud sounds from the hallway pouring in…locker doors closing, sneakers squeaking, annoying voices of my classmates…*man, I hate Harrow High.*

There were two people talking now, standing right in front of my door at the row of porcelain sinks. I tilted my head to the left…down, down, down…until I could make out the shapes of their legs only a few feet away.

If I wanted to, I could take the expression, "knocks their socks off" to a whole other level.

I lowered the gun, aimed it for the back of a tan, fuzzy calf. Closed my left eye.

My finger resting on the trigger, I pressed. It made a small, barely noticeable *click.*

"Bang bang," I mouthed silently.

The gun wasn't loaded. But tomorrow I'd bring some bullets.

Chapter Four

Dakota

Even if I was in the mood for socializing—I wasn't—there was, once again, no one to talk to in my fourth period, Spanish class. I wondered how to say "I'm bored" in Español?

Yawning, I flipped through my paperback textbook, skimming the terms in the glossary until I received my answer. "*Estoy aburrido*," I muttered.

"Miss Densford?" Mr. Thompson called out, his voice strangely feminine for such a hairy, gruff man like himself.

I sat up ramrod straight from my previously slumped position.

"Anything you want to share with the class?" He was grinning like a Cheshire cat. I squeezed my lips together and shook my head nervously.

"Perhaps you would find my class more entertaining if you taught it yourself?" he suggested, raising his eyebrows challengingly.

Getting on your Spanish teacher's shit list on the

first day of high school was never a good idea. *Too late.*

"No sir." I offered a tight, apologetic smile. He turned back around to the whiteboard and when he did, I heard a melodic giggle coming from the back. *How did I miss that poof of red hair and glittering eyes in the back of the room?* It was Mariella, Genevieve's best friend.

I shot a dirty look over my shoulder, and then tried to focus on the droning sound of Mr. Thompson's voice for the remainder of the period. When the class bell rang, I was more than a little relieved. How was I going to make it through an entire school year filled with such boring classes?

School won't be so bad if you're a varsity cheerleader, I reminded myself.

Ronnie played forward on the basketball team. *Perhaps if he saw me on the sidelines in one of those cute little skirts, showing off my cheerleading moves, he'd want me back*, I considered. Even though I wanted him to want me back, I didn't plan on giving him the time of day when he did. He crushed me, simple as that. All I wanted was an opportunity to return the favor.

***

After spending an hour in a class with one of my enemies and a teacher who now hated my guts, I was relieved to see Sydney and Amanda standing right inside the doorway of the gymnasium, which was where Phys Ed was held. In less than two hours, I would return to this exact place for cheerleading tryouts. Thinking about it made me nervous and excited all at the same time.

Amanda and Sydney were waiting for me, and I enjoyed seeing my two friends together, getting along even though they'd just met. "What's up, girls?" I hoped they didn't hear the quiver in my voice.

I took a deep breath, tagging along behind my two friends, who were headed to the girls' locker room to change into their gym clothes. I wasn't a big fan of getting sweaty before tryouts had even begun, and I could only hope that we wouldn't be doing anything too physical on our first day. Cheerleading requires a great deal of athleticism, but I wasn't crazy about sports involving a ball.

We found a spot to change in the far left corner of the locker room, and I retrieved my pair of gym shorts and a plain white t-shirt out of my backpack. It was stuffed to the gills with my athletic wear for tryouts, a handful of hair accessories, my toothbrush, and a small bag of makeup. I planned on fixing up before tryouts. For now, I turned my back to the others and began stripping out of my jeans and Harrow High t-shirt.

I was seriously modest for several reasons. For one, I was short and slightly chubby. You know those girls with the flat, perfect abs? Well, I'll never be one of those girls. And despite my small, curvaceous figure, I'd never had much of a chest. I couldn't help feeling a little ripped off somehow.

I quickly yanked my t-shirt over my head and shimmied my hips into the tiny gym shorts. I kept my eyes down, avoiding the other girls with their nicely toned, athletic physiques. Suddenly, a high-pitched giggle rang out in the locker room. This time it was coming from the queen bee—Queen Bitch is more like it—herself, Genevieve. She was standing in a row of other girls, pointing right at me. I didn't know what she was saying and I wasn't sure I even wanted to know.

I threw my backpack into the locker and jogged out to the gym floor, keeping my eyes on the laces of my gym shoes. I hit a brick wall. Only, it wasn't a wall, it was Ronnie.

"Are you okay, Dakota?" He looked down at me with genuine concern.

"I'm fine." The corners of my lips curved into a smile despite my better judgement. Ronnie had this effect on me. It was the first time he'd looked at me or spoken to me since he'd broken things off at the end of last year. Memories of our short, but sweet relationship came flooding back. He smiled back slightly, and we seemed to be having a moment. Tucking my hair behind my ears nervously, I opened my mouth to speak…

But then I was interrupted by the whipping motion of a bleached blonde ponytail, and a body cutting right between us. It was Genevieve, of course.

Go figure that the one class I have with Ronnie is also the class that I share with Genevieve. That is just my luck on a day like today.

"I'm so glad we're in Phys Ed together, Pooky Bear!" she squealed, grabbing his forearm and leading him off toward the center of the floor. *Pooky Bear? So disgusting!*

"Maybe, if we have time, I'll show you some of my cheerleading moves before tryouts!" she bragged, looking back at me smugly.

At that moment, I wished I had an egg to throw at her glittery, perfectly made up, fake-tanned face. But since this was a gymnasium and not a chicken coop, I headed out to the middle of the gym floor, trying to shake it off.

I saw the net and bundles of balls on each side, and I realized we were playing dodge ball. Another internal groan. Sydney and Amanda jogged over to my side of the net, and we all began stretching our arms and hamstrings. I couldn't keep myself from glancing through the mesh onto the other side of the court. Genevieve and Ronnie were still hanging all over each other. *Barf.*

Our gym teacher, Ms. Lancioni, strolled into the gym, balancing a dodge ball in her right hand and holding a turquoise-colored whistle in the other. In a deep, gravelly voice, she explained the rules of the game, informing my team that it was our turn to throw first. At the sound of her whistle, it was time to throw down.

My own dodge ball was tucked neatly under my arm, and as I continued to glare across the court at Genevieve, I had an uplifting thought. *This may not be a chicken coop, and there may not be eggs to throw, but I have something even better to chuck at her right now, and I can't even get in trouble for it.* I smiled down at my ball happily. Today, dodge ball was my favorite sport.

I'd never had terrific aim when it came to dodge ball, or any sport for that matter, but I'd never been this motivated either. Genevieve wasn't paying attention to the game, and for a moment, she turned her back to the net, leaning over to whisper something to Ronnie. The whistle sounded and that's when I threw it.

My aim was spot on. The ball flew through the air, then drilled her right in the center of her back. She yelped loudly, falling to her knees. Embarrassed, she jumped back up to her feet, brushing nonexistent debris from her knees and upper thighs.

"Who did that?" she howled, the annoying sound of her voice echoing throughout the massive gymnasium. Not backing down, I smiled at her brightly and locked my eyes on hers, enjoying one small moment of revenge. Little did she know, I was planning to achieve a much greater revenge—I was going to get a spot on the squad, no matter what it took to obtain it.

***

The last period of the day was Study Hall. Lucky for me, it was only forty minutes long. The first twenty-five minutes was supposed to be for quiet, individualized study and homework, but the last fifteen minutes was free time. Since I had very little schoolwork from my first day, I planned to rehearse some of my moves in my mind and do some positive self-talk and meditation. Then I planned on spending the last fifteen minutes applying makeup and styling my hair, so that all I'd have to do when the bell rang was put on my gym clothes and wait for tryouts to begin.

I found a decent seat in the back, but didn't see Sydney or Amanda. I was hoping to see them, but in all honesty, I needed some time to relax and calm my nerves. I was just grateful not to see Genevieve or her pal, Mariella. I placed my overloaded backpack under the seat, got comfortable, and then leaned back in my chair, closing my eyes.

My mother had a degree in Social Work, and I couldn't begin to count the number of times she preached about the usefulness of relaxation techniques and positive imaging. I decided to take a page from her book, imagining myself standing alone in the middle of the gym floor.

My feet were planted firmly on the hardwood surface, and I stared straight ahead with a smile. I bent my knees, keeping my back and neck straight as an arrow. Lifting my arms, I pushed off from my toes, and reached my knees up to my chin as I flipped. My feet hit the floor simultaneously. I'd landed my standing back tuck perfectly.

I'd pictured this scenario a thousand times, and in the next scene, the gymnasium erupted with applause. But that part never came because a whiny, high-pitched voice invaded my daydream, and I jerked my eyes open, agitated. The voice belonged to Brittani Barlow, Principal Barlow's daughter, sitting in the desk right next to me.

She was talking to two other classmates about tryouts. "It's going to be an awesome year. I know we'll definitely get to go to the finals in Dallas!" she declared, not caring that everyone around us could hear her. She was talking about one of the biggest cheer competitions in the country, and she was talking about it as though she'd already made the team. I couldn't help it this time. I groaned audibly.

She jerked around, eyeballing me. "Just yawning," I said, rolling my eyes.

"Are you trying out this year, Dakota?"

"Yes, I am," I admitted, waiting for a rude retort.

Instead she surprised me by saying, "Good luck today," and she actually sounded genuine. "Thanks. You too," I grumbled, closing my eyes again.

I tried to conjure up more images of success, but I'd lost interest in it. Mrs. Bartlett was sitting at a stiff metal desk in the front, grading papers. *What could she possibly be grading on the first day already?* I wondered. The important thing was that she was in her own little world, and didn't seem to be paying attention to us. It wasn't free time yet, but I pulled out my makeup bag anyway. I started applying concealer methodically.

I didn't usually wear much makeup, but today was not a typical day. I smiled at myself in the mirror, and again tried to channel my mother's method of positive thinking. But it was hard for me when I looked in the mirror. I was by no means ugly, but I *was* rather plain, with mousy brown hair that hung slightly below my shoulders. It's not curly, but it's not straight either. I had light blue eyes and average skin. I just didn't feel like anything special, really.

But when I put on the glitter, channeled my inner glam girl, and jiggled those pompoms around, I somehow felt like a better version of myself. *I've got to make the team*, I thought determinedly. I finished my makeup and secured my hair in a basic ponytail. I added a thin, black and gold ribbon to it, to represent Harrow's school colors. I couldn't help it—I had to look at the clock. Only a few minutes to go!

It was time to knock their freaking socks off.

Chapter Five

I didn't care how silly I looked…as soon as that final bell sounded, I took off jogging toward the gymnasium. I wanted to be the first one there, so this time I could get dressed in private. Relieved to find the gym empty, I snuck into the locker room, changed quickly, and took one last look at my overall appearance in the mirror. I looked decent. *The important thing today is not how I look, but how well I cheer*, I reminded myself. *You can do this*, I repeated over and over in my mind.

Once dressed, I walked across the gym floor and took a seat on the team bench, the same bench that the home team basketball players would sit on come game night, and the one that Ronnie would place his cute behind on. Basketball tryouts had been held over the summer; I wished cheerleading tryouts were held the same way, but I couldn't get that lucky.

I imagined Ronnie's firm body running up and down the court, his skin glistening with the soft, wavy glow of his sweat. I imagined him leaning forward, tucking my hair behind my ear the way he used to…

I shook the perfect image of him away, my neck and shoulders splotchy from embarrassment. *He is the last person you should be thinking of, Dakota!*

Since I was the first to arrive, I had to sit and watch my competition as they arrived one by one. Unsurprisingly, the returning four girls arrived together. The Triple Ts—Tasha, Tally, and Teresa—were skipping toward the locker room, their arms interlocked, while poor, gawky Monika tagged along behind them. She looked like a lost puppy.

Ashleigh and Brittani were a few steps behind them, and then Genevieve and Mariella strutted in, also arm in arm. They both stuck their noses up at me, disappearing inside the locker room.

Amanda and Sydney were the last to arrive. Finally, someone I was happy to see!

My mind was blank as I waited for the others to change, primp, and come join me on the bench. By the time we were all settled onto the seat, I'd counted eleven of us.

Looking at the numbers, it was pretty close to what I'd expected, except for the addition of Amanda, who totally threw me for a loop by showing up today. I wasn't even sure if she knew a thing about cheering, dance, or gymnastics. *I guess I'll find out soon enough*, I thought, swallowing down a lump in my throat.

Six of us would make it, and five of us would not. I just had to make sure that I fell into the first group.

Chapter Six

When Coach Dolly Davis walked through the door, the gym was so silent you could have heard a pin drop. Even though these girls were my competition, some of them were my friends, and all of us were undeniably nervous. Somehow, I felt a sense of camaraderie with these girls, considering the fact that we were all in the same boat.

Coach Davis was a former NFL cheerleader, with the cheerleading skills to prove it. She's past the age of forty now, but her age didn't put a damper on her beauty. She had soft, auburn curls that hung in ringlets to her chest, bold blue eyes, and a small but athletic figure. When she wasn't coaching, she was busy teaching Western Literature to sophomores. I'd heard she was a nice teacher, considered "easy" by most of her students. Unfortunately, her reputation as a coach differed greatly. She was serious when it came to cheerleading, and rumor had it she was tough, and sometimes cruel, to her squad.

This was her fifth year coaching, and I knew she

was more than a little familiar with the Triple Ts and Monika, as well as Ashleigh, who tried out every year. I still didn't think it was fair, but I reminded myself that nothing ever is, and held my breath as Coach began talking.

"Welcome, girls. Cheerleading tryouts are never easy, as I'm sure those of you who've tried out with me before can attest to. The process usually involves one full day of learning the routine, and then the next day I announce the names of those who have made the team. But…this year, I'm going to do things a little differently. There will still be six girls who make it, but I will also choose a seventh girl to serve as an alternate. If someone is out sick, or God forbid someone sustains an injury, we will have someone as a back-up to fill in when necessary, or as a permanent replacement if need be. I would also like to inform everyone that just because you were on the team last year does not mean you will necessarily make it again. I am a strong believer in fairness, and I want everyone to have a fair shot at making the squad."

She went on, "However, in order to be eligible for the team, all members are required to maintain a 3.0 GPA. If any of you girls don't think you can handle that, please feel free to leave now."

Again, the gym was filled with silence. Everyone stayed put in their seats. "Okay," Coach continued, "I also want to discuss my attendance policy. I will expect each and every girl who makes the team to attend all practices, games, and competitions, unless you have a doctor's note. Each member of the squad is a representative of this school. That means that I expect all of you to be on your best behavior at all times. No drinking, smoking, or drugs. If you get detention, or somehow wind up suspended, believe me when I say this—you *will* be gone from the team."

"No piercings," she added, staring directly at Amanda's eyebrow piercing. "No tattoos, either."

"Now as far as practice is concerned, I will be dividing all of you into three groups to learn a group routine. I will make sure that at least one of our veterans is in each group, as they will be helping to lead you," she said, glancing at Monika and the Triple Ts fondly. Already, I sensed her favoritism for the veterans, but I bit my tongue.

"We'll spend today and tomorrow learning the group cheer. On Wednesday, I'll teach each of you an individual cheer. On Thursday, we will review our individual and group cheers. Friday will be the actual tryouts. Group routines will go first, and then each girl will perform their individual routine. Next Monday, I will announce the six chosen, and the alternate. In addition to learning our routines this week, we will be running a mile every day at the end of practice. If you want to be on this team, then you must prove to me that you're in shape. Any questions?"

I had a million, but I didn't dare raise my hand. Hard work didn't scare me, but I simply couldn't believe I'd have to wait an entire week to find out if I made the team. What a bummer!

"I have a question, Coach Davis." Tasha leaned her head to the side, staring at her bitchy sidekicks. "Which of these freshmen will I be leading in the group routine?" she asked, looking around at the likes of us.

The sideways glance Coach Davis gave her revealed to me that she might not be as fond of Tasha as I thought. *Perhaps I have a shot at beating out the veterans after all*, I thought, perking up in my seat.

"Keep listening and you'll learn the answer." She gave Tasha a stern look.

"First, I will teach the four veterans the cheer, and then I will divide you up into three groups. The veteran girls will then be responsible for teaching their other team members the routine. While I'm teaching Tasha, Tally, Teresa, and Monika, I expect the rest of you to stretch and begin practicing your jumps."

We all nodded dutifully and got down on the floor for stretching. Coach Davis led the veterans to the other side of the gym. Girls were chattering, but I was too nervous, and too focused, to engage in small talk right now. *I have to learn this group routine perfectly tonight, and please, please, please don't let me be on Tasha's team*, I prayed. After smarting off to her earlier today, I felt certain she would find a way to screw me up on the routine if she had the chance.

After Coach Davis taught the veterans the routine, they all returned to the center of the floor, where the rest of us were stretching and doing jumps. Already, I'd noticed that Brittani and Sydney had the highest toe touches and spread-eagles in the bunch. Something else I would have to work on…

"Line up, girls!" Coach Davis puffed on her whistle, causing my ears to ring.

We did as we were told, forming a straight line. I knew she was getting ready to announce the group routine teams, so I took a deep breath and childishly crossed my fingers behind my back.

"The first team will consist of Tasha, Genevieve, Ashleigh, and Sydney." Sydney was my BFF, but I couldn't help thinking—better her than me. Being on a team with Tasha and Genevieve would have been unbearable!

"The second team will consist of Tally, Mariella, and Monika. And the last team will consist of everyone who is left—Teresa, Brittani, Amanda, and Dakota."

Although I didn't like being with one of the Ts or Principal Barlow's daughter, I was glad to be with Amanda, and relieved that I'd avoided the two worst girls in the group. We immediately broke off into our groups and spread out to opposite areas of the gym. My team chose an area close to the locker room. Genevieve and Tasha's group took the center of the floor, of course, while the last team headed off to the far right corner.

I caught Sydney's eye as she trailed behind Genevieve and Tasha. She looked miserable. Ashleigh was on their team too, and she was wearing an expression to match Sydney's. No doubt those two snotty blondes would do everything in their power to outshine Ashleigh and Sydney. I felt so bad for them.

Coach Davis brought each team a compact disc player, and we went to work, learning the routine to music. Teresa demonstrated the entire routine for us while we sat on the floor, studying her moves. It was a complex set of dance movements, cheer motions, and jumps that ended with a basic lift. I could learn the routine…I just needed to learn how to do it better than everyone else.

Chapter Seven

Even though Teresa was one of the evil Ts, she turned out to be, much to my delight, quite a terrific teacher. By the time Coach Davis blew her whistle, everyone on my team knew most of the routine by heart. We were competing as individuals, but in order for this group routine to turn out well, we all had to work together and stay in sync.

Brittani had no problem learning the routine, and Amanda's skills blew me away. She honestly looked like she'd been cheering for years, instead of the beginner she truly was. She even knew how to do a back handspring, though she'd had no formal gymnastics training. I thought about all the years of classes and practicing I'd invested, and couldn't help but feel slightly resentful toward her natural abilities.

"Let's head out to the track and do a mile!" Coach Davis blew that whistle of hers.

The school track was located behind the school building. The eleven of us pushed through the heavy steel doors and began our descent to the starting line of the track. Coach Davis assumed her position beside us, and I respected her for running the mile right along with us. She might be tough, but I liked her.

The whistle sounded and we were off, racing down the long stretch of track, our various types of sneakers pounding against the dirt loudly. I enjoyed the sound of it…it reminded me of being a young girl, racing my friends on the playground at school. I wasn't the fastest runner, but I did have endurance. I could do this mile, no problem. And I wasn't worried about out-running the other girls. After all, this was cheerleading, not track.

I ran at a steady pace, keeping my eyes focused on the lane in front of me. I remembered to control my breathing. By the time I made my way all the way around, I felt exhilarated.

"As soon as you finish, you're free to go!" Coach shouted. She was already finished herself, stretching gracefully in the grass next to the track. She didn't have to tell me twice—I was exhausted.

Sydney and Amanda caught up with me, and we walked together to the front entrance of the school. Sydney's dad was parked out front in his silver Mercedes. "Call me tonight. Lots to discuss," she said breathlessly, jogging off.

I could see my mother parked several cars back from him, waiting faithfully as always. Not only was my mother always on time, but she was usually early. When I cheered in primary and middle school, she never missed a game. Not that she was one of those crazy cheer moms; quite the contrary. She was simply supportive of everything I did, and she wanted me to make the team because she knew how bad I wanted it myself.

I smiled at her through the windshield of her beat-up Toyota Camry. Considering the size of our house, you'd think she would drive something fancier, but she doesn't. She likes her old car just the way it is. I couldn't wait until I had my driver's license and could drive myself around, but deep down, I knew that someday when I was thirty, I would miss having her there to pick me up every day.

Amanda was still standing by my side and I knew she was too proud to ask for a ride. I knew for a fact that her Grandma Mimi wasn't going to leave the house and come pick her up. "Will you ride home with me? Let's talk about tryouts." I opened up the back door of the Camry so she could climb in.

"Hey, Mom!" I greeted her, climbing in beside Amanda. "You don't mind taking Amanda home, do you? She lives just next door," I explained, even though my mom already knew who Amanda was.

"Sure!" she said, in her usual cheerful voice. I could tell that my mom was dying to ask me about tryouts, but I knew she'd wait until after we dropped Amanda off.

"Our group routine is fabulous! I definitely think the four of us will make it!" Amanda exclaimed excitedly. Since Amanda was new, she didn't know much about the four veterans, or Ashleigh's year to finally get a turn, or who Brittani's mother was, so I had the honor of filling her in. I didn't want to bum her out by admitting that our chances were slim, but that was exactly what I did. When I was done talking, she looked as though she might cry.

"I'm sorry," I told her afterwards, the disappointed expression on her face making me feel guilty.

"At least we live close to each other, and can practice together!" she reminded me perkily.

My mother pulled up in front of Amanda's house. Amanda gathered up her backpack. "What the heck do you have in that thing on the first day? It looks so freaking heavy!" I chuckled.

"Thanks for the ride, Mrs. Densford! Bye, Dakota," she said, climbing out of the car.

"We can beat the odds! Don't let my pessimism get you down!" I yelled out the window. She gave me a thumbs up sign.

I knew I needed to practice the group routine, but I was simply too exhausted when I got in. I needed to eat, shower, and solve some pre-algebra problems that I should have completed in Study Hall when I had the chance. Mom ordered pizza while I ran upstairs to take a shower.

The hot water felt good on my sweaty skin, and the lavender smell of my bath soap helped soothe my nerves. I couldn't help it; I started reciting the routine in my mind as I scrubbed my body clean. I wanted to make the team so bad. *We all do*, I reminded myself.

I ran through the entire routine several times before the water went cold. I allowed my hair to air dry while I rushed through the math problems. I finished just in time for the doorbell to ring, announcing the arrival of pizza.

My mom was downstairs waiting for me, laying out paper plates and opening pizza boxes. She'd ordered my favorite garlicky bread sticks and my favorite type of pizza, Italian sausage and mushrooms. I smiled at her graciously. She must have known that I needed this on a day like today.

"Thanks, Mom." I piled my plate with gooey pizza and breadsticks.

I knew my mom was waiting to hear about tryouts, so I went ahead and filled her in. Like always, she was supportive and encouraged me to stay positive about my chances of making the team. It was exactly what I needed to hear at the moment.

Dad was sleeping in his favorite armchair and my baby brother was sleeping too. Mom and I watched one of our favorite shows before we both retired to bed.

Before I could go to sleep though, I had to do one thing. I had to call Sydney. I knew she must be totally bummed about being on a team with the mega bitch and bitch junior.

Even though it was after eleven, I knew she'd be awake. I used the speed dial function on my iPhone to call her, but surprisingly, she didn't answer. So, I did what any girl my age would do—I sent her a text. Ten minutes later, I received a response.

Sydney: I'm tired. Don't feel like talking. See you tomorrow.

I could understand her being tired because I was worn out too, but I got the sense that Sydney was upset with me for some reason. I laid down, almost instantly falling asleep as I wondered why my best friend was always so moody…

Chapter Eight

When I walked out my front door in the morning, I was relieved to see Amanda standing at the end of her grandma's driveway. I hated the idea of her walking all those miles to school. But mostly, I hated the idea of her catching another ride with Ronnie. She was wearing her ***'Kill Your TV'*** shirt again, but I noticed the eyebrow piercing was gone.

"You really do want to be a cheerleader." I grinned at the tiny, reddish mark on her brow that would undoubtedly turn into a scar. "You look better without it," I assured her. She didn't look so sure as she rubbed the spot self-consciously.

"I feel naked without it," she admitted.

My first four periods were just as boring as the day before. I looked forward to seeing Amanda and Sydney at lunch. I wanted to see how Sydney was doing, and make sure she wasn't mad at me for some reason. At lunchtime, she wasn't waiting for me at the same spot.

I entered the cafeteria, scanning the entire length of the lunch line. I saw Amanda in the middle of the line, holding her tray to her chest, chatting up a pair of boys in front of her. Again, I was just glad it wasn't Ronnie. I approached and tapped her on the elbow.

"Hey, girl!" she squealed.

"Can you get me a couple of peanut butter and jelly sandwiches? I need to go find Sydney," I asked. She nodded absentmindedly, turning back to the boys.

I headed into the lunchroom, scanning the circumference of the room, looking for my friend. My eyes naturally landed on Ronnie. If this was *Where's Waldo?*, and he was the star, I'd win every time.

Unfortunately, Genevieve was by his side. And by her side was…Sydney? I couldn't believe it! Why was my best friend hanging out with my arch enemy?

The Triple Ts and Ashleigh were also sitting with them. Ashleigh was sweet to everyone, so that didn't surprise me, but Genevieve and Tasha? And the other Ts? It seemed strange.

I knew I shouldn't go over there, but Sydney was, after all, my best friend. I'd never been hesitant to approach her, and I wouldn't start today.

Genevieve saw me coming, and she leaned in close to Sydney, whispering something in her ear. Sydney immediately looked up at me just as I reached the table.

"Hey, how's it going?" I placed my hands on my hips, instantly feeling foolish. Who was I to say who Sydney could be friends with?

"Fine. We're going over our routine together,

since we're on the same group team," Sydney explained, pointing to Genevieve, Tasha, and Ashleigh. I felt like asking her why the other two Ts were at the table then, but I held my tongue.

"Okay. I'll see you later in Phys Ed," I said, smiling at her.

"Okay, but…" Sydney started to say.

"But what?" I asked, completely baffled by her aloofness.

"It's just…well, Genevieve asked our Phys Ed teacher if we could work on our routine during the entire period, so I might not get to hang out with you at all today." She stared down at her hands, avoiding my gaze.

"I understand." *And I did. I understood exactly what Tasha was doing. She wanted her group of four and her two besties to be the final six, so she was creating a wedge between them and the rest of us.*

I wouldn't mind so much if one of them wasn't my best friend.

Chapter Nine

Sydney had warned me that she might be too busy to talk to me in Phys Ed, and she stayed true to her word. I tried my best not to worry about it. Amanda and I followed Sydney and Genevieve's lead, and we also went off to our own corner of the gym to practice. Most of our other classmates were playing flag football in the center of the gym floor.

As Amanda and I went through the motions of our group routine, I couldn't help but check out Ronnie, who was running with the football in hand, girls swarming around him, playfully trying to grab the flag that was tightly hooked to his belt. When I looked over at Amanda, I saw I wasn't the only one fawning over Ronnie. I groaned.

"What?" Amanda raised her soon-to-be scarred eyebrow at me questioningly.

"We used to date…me and Ronnie," I explained. Honesty is always the best policy, or at least that's what my mother tells me. I figured if I just told her that I still had feelings for him, maybe she would back off.

"Oh, okay," Amanda replied, shrugging slightly. "Let's run through it again," she suggested, overtly changing the subject. We started the group number back from the top.

***

Brittani was waiting for me when I walked into Study Hall. She motioned me over, pointing at the desk beside hers. I had no choice but to take a seat. I guess since we're doing our group routine together, she thought we could be friends.

"So, what do you think about your chances of making the team?" she asked. *Notice how she doesn't seem concerned about her own chances?* I shrugged.

"I think Tasha, Tally, Teresa, and Monika have a definite advantage since they've all been on the team the last three years. I can't see Coach Davis cutting them from the team, especially not their senior year. All we can do is try our best." I was trying to sound optimistic and impartial.

"My mom said that there's no way I won't make the team." Brittani folded her arms over her chest, pleased with herself for some reason. She was wearing the lamest "trying to look like a geek but I'm not" sweater vest.

I couldn't believe she was playing the "my mom is the principal" card! I just couldn't wrap my brain around the arrogance and audacity of this girl!

"Just because your mom is Principal Barlow doesn't mean you're a shoe-in to make it," I retorted, my voice sounding angrier than I would have liked.

"My mom is the reason Coach Davis gets a paycheck, Dakota. Do you really think she's stupid enough to cut me?"

She had a point, but I wasn't about to listen to any more of her bullshit. I turned around in my seat, clenching my teeth.

Perhaps she was trying to psych me out so I'd drop out of the competition, but her antagonism just fueled the fire within me. As far as I was concerned, all conversations with Brittani Barlow were over. She could brag about who her mother was to somebody else.

I was trying to be tolerant of Brittani up until now, but I could no longer see the point. When she leaned forward to say something else, I grabbed my stuff and moved to a seat on the opposite side of the room. All I wanted to do was finish up my homework and count down the minutes until day two of cheerleading tryouts. Brittani watched me strangely, eyes narrowed.

Chapter Ten

Maybe I was anxious about tryouts or maybe it was the extra spicy chimichanga I'd eaten for lunch, but my stomach was doing somersaults. I didn't want to be late to practice, but I had to make a pit stop at the restroom.

I was moving against traffic, kids heading out to catch the bus or get in their cars in the school parking lot, all the while I was struggling to move in the other direction. Finally, I reached my destination.

The bathroom was deserted, quiet. I locked myself in the last stall and willed my stomach to stop cramping. I heard the door open and close, sounds of kids leaving school filtering in from the hallway.

I waited for whoever had come in to enter a stall, but they never did. I sat there, strangely holding my breath. What was I waiting for?

I bent my head down, awkwardly trying to look under the stall for a pair of feet. Just as I did, a pair of boots stopped right in front of my stall door.

I don't know why, but I jerked back suddenly. The hairs on my arms stood up. Quietly, I tucked my legs up, waiting for the weirdo to go away.

I was tempted to bend back down, see if the feet had moved, but I stayed frozen, gripping my knees until my knuckles turned white.

I sat there for so long, I started to wonder if maybe they'd left and I'd just failed to hear them.

Just when I was about to get up and waltz out of the stall, I heard what sounded like heavy breathing through the door.

What the hell?

Anger rising, I jumped off the toilet and smacked my palms against the stall door.

"Get the hell out of here and away from my stall, freak!"

Silence.

But then I heard the boots moving. They seemed to pause in front of the main door, but then finally, I heard it open and close.

I let out a whoosh of breath. I opened the door and walked out, looking around nervously.

Grabbing my backpack, I took off down the hallway. I was going to be late to tryouts.

Chapter Eleven

Day two of tryouts was brutal. The first thing Coach Davis made us do was run suicides up and down the gym floor. After that we did fifty sets of each jump, and one hundred push-ups—not the girly styled push-ups either. In no time, I'd completely forgotten about the psycho-breather in the bathroom. It was probably just some upperclassmen trying to scare me anyway…

By the time we broke off into our groups to practice, we were all exhausted and breathless. However, today was the last day to practice the group routine together before tryouts, because tomorrow we would begin training for individual routines.

We started the group routine with our hands on our hips, and the first several minutes included doing simple kicks and flirty dance moves. But then the routine transitioned to a complex set of running back tucks, and a stunt at the end with Teresa standing with her arms extended in a V on top of mine and Brittani's hands, while Amanda supported the back. It was a pretty tough lift, but we'd been doing it well in our practice sessions.

We ran through the routine several times. It was almost time to do our mile and go home, but we decided to practice it one last time. Our final run-through seemed to go even better than the last, and Teresa's balance was perfect as we lifted her in the final stunt. She held the move for several moments, just like she was supposed to. Normally, we lowered her down properly, allowing her to use our hips as stepping points for getting down.

But suddenly, Brittani let go of Teresa's right foot and took a step back. In what seemed like slow motion, she fell so fast there wasn't enough time for me to react. She hit the floor with a sickening thud, and there was the unmistakable sound of something cracking. I gasped.

She let out a high-pitched scream, grabbing at her ankle desperately from a fetal position on the floor.

I fell to my knees beside her, as did Amanda. "Don't move." I forced myself to look down at her ankle. It was twisted at a bizarre angle and a sizable lump had formed above her foot. No doubt it was broken. At this point, I could only hope there was nothing else broken. She had fallen so fast and hard, and from pretty high up.

"We need an ambulance, Coach Davis," Brittani called out in an abnormally calm voice for such a panicky moment. Coach Davis was already on her cell phone, talking to a 911 operator, while the other girls gathered around Teresa, trying to soothe her pain with kind words and support. I couldn't believe this had happened.

"I did it for you, ya know..." Brittani whispered in my ear.

I spun around, gaping at her. "You...*what*?"

Suddenly, a chill ran up from my spine to the base of my neck. I stood there, staring at Brittani, completely flabbergasted.

"Shhh..." Brittani put a finger to her lips. "I'm helping you out by clearing more space on the team for you, silly," she whispered, smiling strangely. Then she winked at me, her lips curling up into a humorless smile. I stared at her wide-eyed, unable to hide my horror.

Chapter Twelve

Needless to say, Coach Davis let us off the hook when it came to running our mile that day. Teresa was wheeled out on a gurney by two paramedics. We all knew but didn't want to say it out loud—there was no chance in hell she'd be able to cheer this season.

I was still in shock from Brittani's confession, and unsure what to do with the information. I couldn't prove that she dropped her on purpose and I wasn't sure anyone would believe me, anyway.

As Amanda and I climbed into my mom's Camry, I knew my mom could tell that something was wrong simply by looking at my ashen expression.

I told her about Teresa's "accident." I wanted to tell her the truth, but I knew my mom would make me tell Coach Davis if she knew what really happened.

I barely talked the whole way home. "You okay, Dakota?" Amanda asked before climbing out of the back as we pulled up in front of her house. I nodded solemnly, swallowing hard.

"Everyone knows it wasn't your fault, so don't worry." She stepped out, waving goodbye to my mom. I blinked hard, considering her words. Never once had it occurred to me that anyone might hold me responsible for the accident. But I was, after all, supposed to be the one holding Teresa up in the lift and bringing her down safely from the stunt.

That accident made me look bad. *So bad, indeed, it might cost me a spot on the team!* I realized. Instantly, I felt guilty for thinking such selfish thoughts. Here I was worried about something frivolous like cheerleading while Teresa was probably lying in a cast somewhere.

***

I tried to go to bed early. After such a stressful day, I needed to relax and decompress. I also needed to think about what Brittani did and what I should do about it. Once again, I reached the conclusion that there was nothing I could do. I just wished I could tell somebody.

I felt like calling Sydney, but after the way she acted at school today, I didn't see the point. She obviously didn't want to talk to me or she would have made time for me at school. I suddenly had a thought. Maybe I could talk to Amanda. She was right next door after all, and I trusted her not to say anything.

I wondered if she was still awake, or already in bed like me. I got out of bed, pulled my robe tight around me, and walked over to my bedroom window. It was a full moon tonight—not surprising after the day I'd had—but there wasn't a star in the sky. Amanda's house was mostly dark, but the front porch light still shone brightly, illuminating the front yard and entranceway.

I squinted out at the hazy glow, noticing movement in the shadows. That's when I saw Amanda leaning down in front of someone on the stone porch steps. She seemed to be kissing someone. Whoever it was, they were sitting on the steps, and she was leaning down with her face pressed to theirs.

I stood on my tiptoes, squinting into the silvery darkness. When Amanda finally came up for air from the kiss, I could see the sharp outline of his face. I don't know why I was so surprised. It was Ronnie, of course.

Chapter Thirteen

The next day at school, I avoided Amanda like the plague. In fact, I pretty much avoided everyone. At lunchtime, I skipped eating and hid out in the girls' bathroom. I knew I'd regret not eating later, as my stomach was already growling angrily. You'd think I'd be worried about the psycho-breather, but he/she was the least of my concerns when I was dealing with a real psycho, like Brittani Barlow. *How could she do that to Teresa? Why was my best friend giving me the cold shoulder? And why was my new friend making out with my ex behind my back?*

I didn't want to see anyone right now.

I couldn't avoid Amanda any longer by the time our Phys Ed class rolled around. By some miracle, she and I were chosen for different sides in a basketball scrimmage. I avoided all eye contact, trying to sit the bench as much as possible. I couldn't wait for the school day to be over.

To make matters worse, I had to see Brittani in Study Hall next. She immediately came over and tried to chat with me, but I stuck out my hand crisply, stopping her mid-sentence. "If you ever pull a stunt like that again, Brittani, I will—"

It was her turn to cut me off. "You'll do *what*, Dakota? Go tell my mom, the *principal*?" she let out a loud, creepy cackle. *What was wrong with her?*

"I'll tell the police," I answered seriously. That seemed to shut her up. "You could have broken her neck," I hissed.

"Well, I didn't. She got hurt just bad enough to keep her from trying out for the team," Brittani said crudely, biting her lower lip. Then she added, "Don't pretend like you actually liked Teresa. She got what she deserved…"

Somewhere deep inside her, I hoped she felt at least a glimmer of guilt. If not, I was starting to seriously worry about her sanity. I stuck my nose in a paperback and shut out the world again.

When the final bell rang, I made my way down to the gym. Coach Davis was waiting for us. "Listen, girls. I don't want what happened yesterday to ever happen again. Make sure you're using proper dismounting techniques when coming down from a stunt," she warned all of us.

But she was looking straight at me as she said it.

We all nodded our heads in agreement. I felt all hope of making the squad drain out of me. "Now, I want everyone to line up across from each other. We're going to learn the individual routine."

Chapter Fourteen

Even though it was raining, Coach Davis made us run outside on the track before releasing us from practice. I assumed that Amanda would still need a ride home, and I felt a little awkward approaching her, considering the fact that I'd done so well at avoiding her all day. No matter how angry I was at her for kissing Ronnie, I wasn't cruel enough to make her walk six miles home in the rain. *Maybe I should just forgive her. Maybe I'm just being silly*, I scolded myself.

That thought quickly dissipated as I saw her climbing in the passenger seat of Ronnie's Trans Am. He was one of the few freshman boys who already had their license. *Probably because he was held back a grade or two*, I thought bitterly.

Amanda saw me approaching, and she smiled apologetically before pulling his passenger door closed behind her. The Trans Am's tires squealed as they sped off together.

I turned around and ran to my mom's Camry. I didn't want anyone to see the tears forming in the corners of my eyes. I jumped into the back, slamming my backpack down on the floorboard. I held my face in my hands, willing the tears to go away.

Moments like this, I wished I wasn't so transparent and my mom couldn't read my mind. "That girl's had a hard life." She looked back at me in the rearview mirror, her eyes soft. I guess she saw what happened.

"So, since she's had a hard life, I just have to let her take my boyfriend?" I spat. My mom was quiet for several minutes before saying gently, "Remember, Dakota, he's not your boyfriend."

The words hurt, but they rang true. My mom was right. Ronnie wasn't my boyfriend—he was Genevieve's, and when she found out about Amanda, if she hadn't already, she was going to make Amanda's life a living hell.

"When you get older you'll realize that sometimes having a friend is more important than having a boyfriend," mom added.

"I guess you're right," I replied sulkily, sinking down in my seat.

Chapter Fifteen

When I walked through the doors of Harrow High, I had a little pep in my step. I'd stayed up late practicing the group and individual cheer routines. I felt confident, deciding to convert all of my negative energy into determination to succeed at tryouts. I didn't need to waste my energy or time worrying about Ronnie, or anyone else for that matter.

Today would be our last practice before tryouts on Friday, and that was all I was focused on. I aced my Biology and Pre-Algebra exams, and even made a new friend in American History. His name was Andy McGraw, and we ended up getting stuck together for a history project on Joan of Arc after everyone else had already picked partners. He was tall and lanky, with flashy red hair and a patch of freckles on his nose and cheeks. He seemed to turn every little thing into a joke, which was fine because I needed more comedy in my life. I didn't really see him as a prospect for dating, but considering how poorly things were going for me in the friend department, I could use an extra one of those.

When lunchtime rolled around, I didn't even bother looking for my friends. I jumped in the lunch line, selecting random foods that looked appetizing. Skipping lunch yesterday was a terrible idea, and I decided not to do that again. I needed a high energy level for the last practice today, and eating well would help.

I gave the cashier two dollars and eighty-three cents, and I stepped into the main lunchroom, which was filled with rows and rows of lunch tables. Now that I was friendless, I knew what it felt like to have nowhere to sit. *The next time I see someone looking around for someone to sit with, I swear I'll wave them over, because this is not a good feeling*, I decided.

Instantly, I spotted Sydney at Tasha and Genevieve's table again. I tried to catch her eye, but she was too caught up in whatever topic they were discussing. On the other side of the room, I saw Brittani and a group of preppy girls who looked just like her. She caught me looking and waved. *Yuck. That girl is crazy.* I didn't see Amanda anywhere. But that was probably a good thing.

"Hey, you," said a voice from behind me, causing me to jerk with surprise. Much to my delight, it was Andy from American History. "Do you want to sit with the cool kids?" He raised his eyebrows, flashing that little half-smile I couldn't help but adore.

"Who are these cool kids you speak of?" I asked curiously, unable to hold back a smile myself.

"Well, it's *one* cool kid, actually, and you're looking at him! How lucky do you feel right now?"

Andy was such a clown, but I loved the lighthearted feeling I got from just being around him. We found a semi-abandoned spot at one end of a center lunch table. He chewed with his mouth open and told cheesy jokes, but for some reason, when I was around him I forgot about everything that was bothering me. Tryouts, my failing friendships, the pressure, the psycho-breather, Teresa's accident…

Speaking of Teresa, she stumbled inside the lunchroom, trying to juggle the complicated task of using crutches and carrying her lunch tray simultaneously.

She looked so pitiful, and I immediately jumped up to hurry over to her side. Taking the tray from her hands, I led her over to the table with me and Andy. "How are you feeling?" I asked, afraid to hear the answer.

"I'm okay. It's just a pain using these things," she said, nodding down at the crutches. She leaned them against the side of the table and hopped on one foot over to her seat, plopping down on the bench.

"Is your leg broken?" I winced at her cast.

"Only in three places," she joked, prying open a carton of juice with her teeth.

"I'm so sorry, Teresa." I stared at the food on my tray, watching mac n' cheese blur together as I fought back tears. I needed to eat, but my stomach was in knots again.

"I'll let you guys talk. I need to get going to my next class," Andy said, waving at Teresa politely and winking at me.

"See you later," I called out after him, and I really hoped I would get to see him later.

"It wasn't your fault," Teresa said, catching me by surprise.

"I know. But I'm still sorry it happened. I hate that you got hurt…"

"No, that's not what I mean." Putting her hand on my arm, she gave it a light squeeze. I set down my fork and looked at her expectantly. I was worried that I knew what was coming next…

"I know Brittani did it on purpose. I felt her let go of my foot, and then I saw the smile on her face when I hit the floor." I couldn't believe she actually knew and was staying so calm about it!

"We need to go to Coach Davis and tell her the truth," I said, prepared to find the coach and do it right then, but Teresa just shook her head.

"This has been a real wake up call for me, Dakota. I mean, I've been pretty mean to other girls over the years, and maybe if I were in Brittani's shoes, I would have done the same thing." She shrugged nonchalantly.

I didn't know what to say to that, so I just sat there staring at her. "And now Tasha and Tally won't talk to me, just because I'm not going to be a cheerleader anymore." She rolled her eyes angrily. Now *that* piece of information did not surprise me.

"Just promise me you'll beat them for me," she pleaded, turning back to me and taking my hand in hers.

"I'll do my best," I promised.

Chapter Sixteen

The bell for fifth period was moments away, so I went to my locker to get my Spanish book. Andy was leaning against it, waiting for me. "I got to get to class," I warned him, motioning for him to move aside so I could open my locker. The talk with Teresa had really bummed me out, and I was feeling guilty as hell.

"That's okay. I have to get going too. I just wanted to see if…maybe you would like to hang out today after school?" Andy scratched the back of his neck nervously.

"I would love to, but I can't. I have cheerleading practice after school." I gave him an apologetic smile.

"How about after practice?" he suggested hopefully, unwilling to give up just yet.

I felt terrible for saying no again, but tonight was my last night before tryouts, and I needed to practice for the big day and get a good night's rest. I told him that, trying not to feel guilty when I saw the disappointed look on his face.

"How about we hang out this weekend?" I suggested instead. He perked back up. I reached for his left hand and pulled it toward mine. Using an ink pen, I scribbled my number on the back of his hand in big, loopy numbers.

"Gotta go." I slipped my backpack over my shoulder and took off down the hall.

I planted my butt into my seat just as the bell rang for Spanish. Thank God I wasn't late; the last thing I needed to do was tick off Mr. Thompson again. I was already on his bad side.

Speaking of being late, I caught a glimpse of two people through the open bay window, running through the courtyard frantically. They were obviously late getting back to class. I'd recognize that unusual haircut and handsome bod anywhere. It was Amanda and Ronnie.

So, that explains why she wasn't at lunch, I realized, rolling my eyes resentfully. If Amanda did make the cheerleading squad, I could see her getting into trouble fast with Coach Davis. Students weren't allowed to be outside or off the premises during lunch hours.

Oh well. It's none of my business what they do anymore, I thought with a sigh. As much as I tried not to let it bother me, I stewed on it the whole period, clenching my teeth as I imagined them together.

Chapter Seventeen

The rest of my classes flew by, and when the final bell chimed, I made my way to the gym for day four of tryouts. Sydney was standing inside the doors, leaning up against a wall padded with gym mats. *Probably waiting for her new pal, Genevieve.* I strolled right past her, heading to the locker room to change.

"Dakota, wait!" Sydney jogged to catch up with me. I turned to face her, defensively placing my hands on my hips.

"Look, I'm sorry. And I miss you," she said, her eyes brimming with tears. I let out a deep sigh.

"I miss you too. I don't understand why you've been acting this way." I searched her face for some sort of explanation.

"I guess I was jealous about you hanging out with Amanda. And Genevieve has been doing everything in her power to keep me by her side. She said that if I want to make the team I need to stick by her, and do all of my practicing with her," she revealed, her face reddening in embarrassment.

"I'm a nervous wreck about tryouts tomorrow, and I really need my best friend back."

"I need you too." I reached out and gave her a hug.

We stood there for several moments, enjoying our embrace. *Thank God I finally have my friend back*, I thought cheerily. However, our sweet little moment was interrupted by the sound of Coach Davis's whistle.

"Line up for suicides, girls!"

We all groaned in unison.

We headed over to the left-hand side of the court. Genevieve was staring at Sydney, giving her the evil eye for talking to me. *What a crazy bitch!* I thought, shaking my head and staring down at my feet, ready to get this running over with.

As we waited for another whistle to signal our start, Amanda came running into the gym. "Sorry I'm late!" She dropped her bag on the sidelines. She scurried over to where we were standing, joining us on the line.

"Since you were late, your teammates can thank you by doing an extra fifty push-ups, on top of the hundred they already have to do." There were more groans all around, and Amanda looked mortified.

"Coach?" Genevieve stepped forward, raising her hand like she was in class.

"Yes, Genevieve?" There was a note of irritation in Coach's voice.

"On behalf of everyone here, I just want to let you know that Amanda left the school premises with a boy today during our lunch hour. I don't mean to be a tattle tale, but I don't want someone who breaks school rules on *my* team. I thought you had a right to know," she said, stepping back in line. She looked from side to side, smiling at the girls standing next to her. She couldn't wipe that smug look off her face even if she tried.

I closed my eyes, squeezing them tightly. I braced myself for Coach's reaction to this piece of information. Even though I was ticked off at Amanda for hanging out with Ronnie, I didn't really want to see her get in trouble or kicked out of tryouts. I stole a glance at her face. Amanda's face was crimson, and she was staring at her feet shamefully.

Coach Davis's eyes traveled up and down the line of girls before she opened her mouth to speak. "Like you said, Genevieve, this *is* a team. And although I understand not wanting one of your possible fellow squad members to break the rules, I also suspect that your team members don't want to cheer with someone who tries to get her own teammates in trouble." That shut Genevieve up real quick.

Hooray for Coach Davis! I enjoyed seeing someone stand up to Genevieve. I had to stifle a laugh. *It serves her right,* I thought, wearing my own smug smile. I was starting to like Coach Davis more and more.

Chapter Eighteen

Although part of me had forgiven Amanda, I still felt angry when I saw her riding home with that douche bag again. *I wonder what she sees in that guy*, I thought glumly. But then I remembered that I too, fell for Ronnie's charm once upon a time.

I hopped into the car with my mom and filled her in on the day's events. I don't know why, but I was starting to feel like the only reliable friend I had was my mother. "Do you want to go get some sushi?" she offered, looking back at me with a smile.

I needed to go home and practice, but I loved sushi, and time spent doing anything that didn't involve cheerleading or cheerleading-related drama sounded good right then. "Let's do it," I told her, returning the smile.

***

After dinner with my mom, she spent two hours watching me practice my routines. "You know the routines perfectly, honey. You should try to get some rest tonight," she encouraged. I knew she was right, and I had to admit that my body was spent after all of the running, lifting, and jumping this week. Not to mention all of the stress.

I took a shower and packed my favorite sparkly leotard and shorts for tryouts tomorrow. Now that tryouts were less than twenty-four hours away, I could feel my body buzzing with excitement. I decided to call Sydney to wish her luck. I was so glad to hear the sound of her voice. Hell, I was just glad she was taking my calls again.

"What's up?" she asked in her usual chipper tone. I could hear her chewing gum noisily on the other end. I could picture her, lying on her Justin Bieber bedspread, twirling her long, dark locks around her pointer finger.

"Not much. I've been practicing all night, and now I'm trying to go to bed. But I'm just too excited to sleep!" I admitted.

"I know what you mean! I've had butterflies in my stomach all week!" she said excitedly.

"So, tell me your predictions. Who do you think will make the team?"

"Hmm…" she said, taking her time to think it over. "Well, *us* of course!" She giggled into the phone.

"I also think the veterans will make it—Tasha, Tally, and Monika. And then for the last spot, and I hate to say this because I know you don't like her, but I think Genevieve will make it. She's really not that bad, Dakota. She's nice once you get to know her…" she said softly.

I wanted to stick a finger down my throat and

gag when I heard her defending Genevieve. Yuck! But I did hope she was right about her and I both making the team. “So, can you believe that Amanda skipped school with Ronnie today? Genevieve dumped his ass today,” Sydney confided.

“If you ask me—he dumped her first. He’s been seeing Amanda for a while now,” I responded, letting out a chuckle as I imagined the look on Genevieve’s face when she realized that someone had stolen her guy for once, and not the other way around.

“Amanda and Ronnie have been hanging out for *a while* now?” Sydney inquired angrily. I realized then that I’d said too much, but Sydney was my best friend and I trusted her. I knew that even if she and Genevieve were friends now, she would remain loyal to me.

“Don’t say anything, but I saw him over at her house a couple of nights ago. They were kissing outside. I was mad at her at first. But honestly, I’m sort of over him.” As I said it, I realized it was the truth. Finally, I was getting over that douchebag!

“I’m glad to hear that, Dakota, because he’s an asshole,” she said, sighing loudly into the phone. We talked for a few more minutes, then said our goodbyes.

Even though I was tired, sleep eluded me. I read an eBook on my Kindle until I finally drifted asleep with my head tilted down over the screen.

***

I woke with a start. *Tryouts today!* But then I

suddenly realized that it was still dark outside and my alarm wasn't going off. *What the hell?* I took a peek at my Hello Kitty alarm clock. It was only one-thirty in the morning. I groaned loudly, falling back against my pillows and closing my eyes.

I heard the distant sounds of people shouting outside. I jerked back up to a sitting position, pushed my blankets aside, and tiptoed over to the window. Looking through a gap in the curtains, it took a moment for my eyes to adjust. But then I saw what was causing the noises outside.

There were three people wearing Halloween masks—a werewolf, a vampire, and a Frankenstein. Frankenstein was throwing eggs at Amanda's house, while the other two were tossing toilet paper onto the lawn and strewing it up in the trees.

I didn't know what I should do, so I just stood there watching, trying to figure out who these masked vandals were. Based on the body shapes, I had a good idea. The lights inside Amanda's house remained dark, so they must not have known what was going on. But right on cue, the front door to the house swung open wildly, and crazy Grandma Mimi charged out into the yard, wearing granny panties and an untied robe.

The moment would have been hilarious if it wasn't for the shotgun in her hand. Luckily for the three vandals, Mimi was a bad shot, because she pointed the barrel of the gun straight toward them and pulled the trigger. *Bang!* But it sounded more like a pop…

My ears were ringing as I jerked back from the windowsill.

Peeking back out, I saw the three vandals running away like someone had lit a fire under their rear ends. Actually, someone almost did.

The sound of the blast had rattled my windows. I squatted down and kept watching until Mimi retired back into the house. I couldn't hold it in anymore. I burst into a fit of giggles.

Chapter Nineteen

I was pleasantly surprised to see Amanda standing at the bus stop the next morning. *I guess good ol' Ronnie didn't follow through with giving her rides to and from school*, I thought happily. I couldn't help but notice how great Amanda looked. She had flecks of glitter spread over her cheeks, and her nails were painted perfectly, sporting Harrow's school colors.

"Whoever taught you how to paint your nails sure did a fine job." I let out a long whistle. She smiled halfheartedly.

"Yes, you did," she admitted. "You look cute too," she said stiffly, pointing at my curly ponytail, which was tied up with a gold ribbon. I also had glitter to put on my face for tryouts, but I was going to wait until Study Hall to put it on.

Amanda was staring at me intensely with an odd expression on her face. "Did you guys have a late night last night?" I asked, giving her a look that said I knew about the vandalism. She narrowed her eyes at me suspiciously.

"You don't honestly think it was me, do you?" I gasped, taken aback. "I wouldn't do that to you, Amanda. Or anyone, for that matter. I saw three people with Halloween masks throwing eggs and toilet paper. The sounds woke me up. I couldn't see their faces, but I knew they were girls by looking at their bodies, obviously," I told her, speaking fast so I could quickly dispel any wild ideas she had of me participating in something like that.

"It's one thing for people to mess with me, but I won't let anyone mess with my grandma," she said, looking straight ahead with a hardened expression on her face. "I'm pretty sure your pal, Sydney, was one of them." She turned back to face me angrily.

I shook my head. "No way. Sydney wouldn't do something like that. And I talked to her on the phone last night! She was home, and getting ready to go to bed when we spoke."

But I wasn't sure if I believed it myself. Sydney had been hanging around with Genevieve and her pals lately…

"Yeah, *right*. And I guess you didn't tell anyone about Ronnie coming over the other night, either?" She crossed her arms over her chest. When she saw the shocked look on my face, she smiled.

"There was a note in our mailbox this morning, telling my Grandma that I've been hooking up with Ronnie at night while she's asleep. And guess what? It was signed **'Dakota Densford—Your Concerned Neighbor.'**"

My mouth fell open in surprise. I was utterly speechless. "I didn't write that, Amanda! I would never do that!" I shouted, still confused about how a note with my name on it winded up in her grandma's mailbox.

"My grandma was so upset about the vandalism and the note she told me that I may have to go back home to live with my junkie mom. Thanks a lot," Amanda said bitterly, climbing on the bus as it squealed to a stop in front of us.

Chapter Twenty

Today we were learning principles of chromosomal inheritance in Biology. I really should have been listening, but my mind was spinning and my feelings were hurt. Only a fool wouldn't understand the truth behind Amanda's accusations this morning—Sydney betrayed me. I was the only person who saw Amanda and Ronnie's secret nighttime rendezvous, and the only person I revealed that secret to was Sydney.

I wasn't sure if Sydney was the one who actually wrote Amanda's grandma the fake note and signed my name, but she was the one who caused it to happen, I had no doubt about that. I could imagine Tasha and Genevieve egging someone's house, but I never thought Sydney would participate in something like that. I didn't think she would break her word, and run and tell Genevieve about Amanda, either.

I let out a sigh, frustrated. At least I had tryouts to look forward to today.

When I walked into American History, I was

happy to see Andy waiting for me. I took a seat next to him, tossing my backpack under my chair. He immediately started blabbing my ear off about a YouTube video with a dancing monkey, and I welcomed the distraction. He was so animated and lively as he described every little detail about the video and tried to demonstrate the monkey's dance moves. After a while, I tuned out his voice and just stared at his goofy smile dreamily. Thanks to him, I was starting to feel a little bit better.

Chapter Twenty-One

I had a turkey sandwich on rye bread, with chips and a pickle for lunch. After days of having a nervous stomach, I suddenly felt ravenous. Andy sat beside me, watching me pig out with an appreciative smile.

"Are you nervous about tryouts today?" He used a finger to swipe bread crumbs off my sleeve. I looked at him wondrously. *How did we go from being classroom acquaintances to acting like boyfriend/girlfriend? And why did I like it so much?*

"I'm feeling okay. Thanks for asking." I grinned at him between bites.

Even though I dated Ronnie for nearly six months, he never once asked me a question that solely had to do with me and my interests. I hadn't realized that until just then.

Ronnie's a jerk, and it's a good thing he dumped me when he did, I realized. Ronnie deserved a girl like Genevieve, and they should have stayed a couple.

Speaking of Ronnie's many girlfriends, I looked around the room for Amanda. I still felt bad about her house getting vandalized, but I was hurt that she actually thought I would throw eggs at her house or write a note like that to Grandma Mimi. We hadn't known each other very long, but thus far, I'd been a loyal friend to her. She was the one, after all, who continued to pursue Ronnie, even though she knew that it upset me. *Maybe I should be the one who is angry*, I thought decidedly, finishing the last bite of my pickle.

I finally caught sight of Amanda. She was sitting toward the far end of the cafeteria, chatting with a group of girls I didn't recognize. Several of them looked alternative like her. *Maybe it's for the best that we both find new friends*, I thought glumly.

"I hope you make the team, Dakota," Andy said, bringing my attention back to him.

"I hope so too. I want it so bad. This is all I've ever dreamed of, cheering on the varsity squad for the Harrow Dragons. If I make the team, will you come to some of the games to watch me?" I gave him a hopeful smile.

He surprised me by bursting into a fit of laughter.

"What's so funny?" I stared at him with a confused expression.

"You still don't know, do you?" he asked, shaking his head with a grin.

"Know *what*?" I punched him in the shoulder playfully. Sometimes he could be annoying and cute all at the same time. Maybe that's why I was starting to like him.

"I'm on the basketball team, silly. I made the team during summer tryouts. So, my answer to your question is *yes*. I will be more than happy to come to all of your games and watch you cheer for me on the sidelines." He winked at me adorably.

I couldn't believe it! He was on the team and I didn't even know it!

"You can pick your jaw up off the table now." He nudged me, still smiling. I closed my mouth and smiled back.

This was great news, and now I wanted to make the team more than ever! I couldn't help imagining myself cheering on the sidelines as Andy ran up and down the court, scoring the winning points. That would be so exciting! And now I was more motivated than ever to make the squad.

Chapter Twenty-Two

As though this day had not been filled with enough surprises, Mr. Thompson sprung us with a pop quiz in Spanish. Considering the fact that tryouts were today, I'd spent very little time studying Spanish this week, or any other subjects for that matter. For the quiz, we had to conjugate a list of ten verbs. I struggled with a few of the irregular ones, but lucky for me, I took Spanish in middle school, so I could still recall some of the verbs that I'd learned previously.

Next was Phys Ed. I wasn't looking forward to seeing anyone in that class—Ronnie, Genevieve, Amanda, or Sydney. Honestly, I was ready for the day to be over. I needed to get through tryouts so I could head home to take a long, much needed nap.

When Ms. Lancioni announced that we were going outside today to run on the track, I was overcome with joy. If any of those four came near me, I'd simply run away from them.

But I couldn't avoid Sydney for long, and she caught up with me on my second lap. "I thought everything was cool between us last night. Why are you acting mad at me all of a sudden?" She tried to match my pace. I halted and started jogging in place so Ms. Lancioni wouldn't yell at me for slacking off.

"I don't really want to get into this with you right now," I warned her.

"Get into *what*?" There was a trace of annoyance in her voice.

"I know you went and told Genevieve about Amanda and Ronnie. I know that you, or one of Tasha's minions, wrote that note with my signature on it. And I also know what you guys did to Amanda's grandma's house."

"What note?" Sydney was biting her lower lip nervously. Out of all the things I'd just said, the only thing that confused her was the part about the note? *That's a telling sign.*

"So, then I guess you're admitting that you told Tasha and Genevieve, and what you all did to that poor old lady! You're just lucky you didn't get shot, Sydney!"

"I don't know what you're talking about!" she declared defensively. She turned away huffily and jogged away from me down the track.

"Good riddance!" I shouted after her.

Chapter Twenty-Three

When I walked into Study Hall, I was still reeling from the news that Andy had given me at lunch. I couldn't believe he was on the varsity basketball team! I wondered how well he knew Ronnie. *Ugh.* I pushed *that* thought aside and slid into my seat in the back.

All I had to do was make it through this class and then I could finally go to tryouts. This is what I'd been waiting for all week long. My whole life, actually…

Even though I was bummed about my fights with Amanda and Sydney, I felt confident about tryouts. I was ready to do the group and individual routines. Because of Teresa's "accident," we had to eliminate the stunt at the end altogether. Although that meant the routine was slightly easier for my group, it made me a little worried because I wouldn't get to showcase my lifting skills like the other two groups. We had decided to end the routine with a simple set of toe touches. It wasn't our fault that Teresa couldn't perform, so I didn't think Coach Davis would hold it against us.

Actually, the alterations to the routine were *somebody's* fault, I thought, looking over at Brittani. I narrowed my eyes at her. She was sitting two rows over from me, and was busy fixing her makeup for tryouts. I pulled out my own compact mirror and a small tube of glitter. I smoothed lotion onto my face and waited several minutes for it to dry. Then I squeezed some glitter onto my finger and started dabbing it onto my cheek bones.

I'd never been very good at putting on makeup, and when it came to applying glitter, I always struggled with putting it on my eyelids. I dug a cotton swab out of my makeup bag and tried using it to put the glitter on my eyes without any clumping. My hands were shaky, probably because I was nervous about tryouts.

After I'd finished, I held up the mirror to see how well I'd done. My eyes were a clumpy disaster. I groaned, pulling out a pack of wet wipes and Kleenex to wipe it off. "Please let me help," Brittani purred, plopping down backwards in the chair in front of me. We were face to face, and I shuddered. I couldn't help it; she gave me the creeps.

"I don't want any more of your *help*," I said, clutching my eye, which now had a piece of glitter inside it. *Ouch!* Brittani unzipped her makeup bag, and leaned forward with a wet wipe, helping me remove the makeup. Then she applied a thin coat of eye shadow primer by Urban Decay.

"What color is the outfit you're wearing?" She

studied my face intently.

"Purple," I grumbled.

She took out an awesome eye shadow palette with a range of glittery violet shades. She smoothed it on with steady hands, then dabbed more glitter across each lid. When she held up the mirror for me to see the result, I had to admit it looked great. It pained me to say it, but I did anyway. "Thank you, Brittani." I choked out the words.

For the next ten minutes, I couldn't take my eyes off the clock. I took a deep breath and closed my eyes as the second hand approached its destination. I could almost hear the sound of its ticking reverberating in my head. Just when I couldn't stand the wait one second longer, the bell rang. Show time!

Chapter Twenty-Four

I quickly changed into my purple leotard and shorts, then made my way over to my seat on the bench. The bench was already full with the other hopefuls, and everyone seemed to be sitting next to their respective group members. I took a seat next to Amanda. I tried to catch her eye to wish her luck, but she was staring straight ahead at the padded walls, her lips pursed nervously. She was wearing a sparkly, rainbow-colored leotard. She looked fabulous.

Sydney was sitting at the other end of the bench. Unsurprisingly, she was sitting next to Genevieve and Tasha. She too looked great in a stretchy red sports top and matching shorts that we'd picked out together weeks ago. That trip to the mall seemed so long ago. Now we were barely speaking…

Mariella Martin was wearing a sequin-covered, green leotard that looked nothing short of perfect in conjunction with her bright red hair. Genevieve and

Tasha were wearing matching two-piece outfits that basically looked like slutty bathing suits. *Yuck.*

But the award for strangest outfit had to go to Brittani. She was wearing cotton-fibered shorts over a stretchy leotard covered in pictures of small kittens. "I love kittens," she said defensively, when one of the girls rudely asked why she'd picked it.

The other girls—Tally, Monika, and Ashleigh—were wearing similar variations to the rest of us. Our outfits may have been different, but our expressions were the same—every single one of us looked nervous.

When Coach Davis walked in, I think all of us were holding our breaths. She took a few minutes to get the music for the routines ready, and then she took a seat in a plastic straight-backed chair that gave her a perfect view of the center gym floor.

"The first group who will do their routine is Group Three," she announced, glancing down at a notepad on her lap. She made a few scribbles with a red ink pen. Seeing her there with that notepad was downright intimidating, and hearing my group number called first was not something I'd expected.

However, I jumped to my feet enthusiastically, and followed my two group members out to the middle of the floor.

Since Teresa was no longer in our group, I took my spot in the center, while Amanda and Brittani stood across from each other, forming a row behind me. I placed my hands on my hips and took a deep breath, waiting for the music to begin. Coach Davis did a three count, and then she pressed play on the compact disc player.

The steps to the routine came easily, and I performed them just as I had in practice. Only this time it was the real thing! I stayed on rhythm with the music and hit my jumps perfectly, all the while keeping a smile on my face. At the end, the other girls on the bench clapped with muted enthusiasm. Coach Davis gave us a curt nod, making several notes on her pad. I wished I knew what she was thinking, but I honestly had no clue since she didn't offer us any feedback.

"Group one, you're up!" she called next, looking toward Tasha on the bench. The next group took their places in the center floor, while my group took a relieved seat on the bench. Tasha and Genevieve were standing in the back of the formation, while Sydney and Ashleigh made up the front. Even though I was mad at Sydney, I couldn't help rooting for her. I wanted my best friend to succeed. I crossed my fingers behind my back, watching anxiously from the bench.

Just like when it was my group's turn, Coach Davis did a three count and turned the music on. Immediately, I realized that something was very wrong with their routine. Tasha and Genevieve seemed to be doing the steps perfectly, their movements the same as my group had just done and we'd all learned. But Sydney and Ashleigh were in the front, doing their own separate routine. The moves they performed were childlike and unflattering.

Several girls on the bench snickered. I covered my face with my hands, unable to watch the train wreck unfolding before me. But I couldn't help it; I had to peek to see what was going on.

As I watched Sydney perform the wrong motions, it suddenly occurred to me why Genevieve and Tasha had been keeping Sydney and Ashleigh isolated from everyone else. They had obviously been teaching them the wrong routine!

Obviously, they wanted to sabotage Sydney and Ashleigh's chances of making the squad. If Sydney and I hadn't been fighting this week, we would have been practicing at home together, and she would have figured out the routine she had learned was incorrect. Sydney thought that Tasha and her buddies wanted to be her friends, but she was dead wrong.

At the end of their routine, Genevieve and Tasha grinned at each other mischievously, shooting knowing glances at their pals, Tally and Mariella on the bench. This whole thing was obviously a set up.

"Sydney and Ashleigh! Is that the routine you were taught by your team leader, Tasha?" Coach Davis jumped to her feet angrily. Sydney's smile faded, replaced with a look of confusion. I suppose she thought each group had their own version of the group cheer because she still didn't seem to realize what was going on. She looked around at her team members questioningly.

"Hey, it's not my fault those two couldn't learn the steps! I showed them the routine a million times! And Genevieve mastered the routine just fine," Tasha whined. She looked over at Genevieve, a devilish grin spreading across her face.

Coach Davis walked across the floor, stopping inches away from Tasha's face. "I know you orchestrated this, Tasha. It was *your* job to lead these girls, not *mis*lead them by teaching them the wrong routine!"

Everyone on the bench stiffened at the sound of the Coach's voice. Her face was beet red, and I'd never seen her look so angry. "I'm sorry, Coach," Tasha said, a sickeningly fake, apologetic smile on her face.

"I want you out of here! You are cut from the tryouts!" Coach shouted, surprising us all as she pointed a finger at the exit doors of the gym.

No one was more surprised than Tasha herself. Her jaw nearly hit the floor.

"But…"

"No buts. Out!" Coach Davis commanded.

Tasha looked around at her sidekicks, as though she actually expected someone to come to her defense. Throwing up her hands in disgust, she strolled over to the sidelines to retrieve her bag and stomped noisily out of the gym.

During the whole ordeal, I hadn't moved an inch. I was still in shock. The infamous head T of the Triple Ts was no longer in the running for the varsity squad. I didn't think any of us could have predicted that, not in our wildest dreams! With her out of the running, and Teresa out due to injury, my chances of actually making the team were looking better and better…but I did feel bad for Sydney.

Everyone on the bench started talking all at once. Coach Davis put an end to that. "Is this a gossip session or do you girls want to try out for this squad?" she shouted, instantly shushing us all. "Next group!"

Tally, Monika, and Mariella got into position and started their routine when the music sounded. This time, everyone completed the same routine, thankfully. As I watched Monika and Tally walk back to the bench, I realized they were the only two left of the original squad. I honestly couldn't believe my luck!

Coach Davis began calling our names one at a time to perform the individual cheer. I was glad not to be first this time. Ashleigh was the first to have a turn. Although I was hoping she would do well because this was her junior year, she did make a few mistakes. Brittani went second and was followed by Tally, Mariella, Amanda, and Monika. Everyone seemed to perform well.

Then I heard my name. I walked to the center of the floor, facing Coach Davis again. I smiled confidently and performed the cheer without any mistakes. Genevieve and Sydney were the last to go, and their routines were flawless as well. *I have absolutely no idea who's going to make it*, I realized.

"Girls, please take a seat!" Coach Davis called out. Those who were not sitting already quickly made their way to their seats. Coach Davis stood in front of us, her arms clasped behind her back. "I want to congratulate all of you on a job well done. I wish I could choose all of you, but we only have six sets of uniforms and pompoms," she admitted, sounding nice and apologetic for the first time all week. "I will spend some time thinking about my decision over the weekend. The names of the six girls who make it will be announced over the intercom at some point during the day on Monday. The girls who do make it, please stay after school on Monday and meet me in the gym to pick up your pompoms and get fitted for your cheerleading uniforms. Thanks to all of you for trying out. You are dismissed!"

Chapter Twenty-Five

I expected the weekend to drag by slowly, because I wanted Monday to get here so badly, but it actually went by rather fast. Mom took me and my little brother out to the movies on Saturday. She was trying to distract me from worrying about making the team, and I loved her for doing so. It was one of those animated movies that were supposed to be for children, but even adults couldn't help loving them. My dad had to work so he couldn't join us, but we took baby Vincent. I loved my little brother to death, but he was only a year old, and he was fussy throughout the film. Nevertheless, I enjoyed the family time and distraction from the torture of waiting to find out Coach Davis's decision.

On Sunday, Andy called. I was pleased to hear from him. Right off the bat, he asked how the tryouts went. Since I didn't have many friends to consult with these days, I spilled all of the gossip to him. I told him about Tasha getting kicked out of tryouts for sabotaging her group members, and we discussed my chances of making the team.

"I have a good feeling you're going to make it," he assured me sweetly.

"Thank you for believing in me."

There was a moment of awkward silence, and then he said, "So, I was wondering if you'd like to come over and work on our history project?" His voice was shaky, hesitant. His nervousness was adorable!

"I'd almost forgotten about Joan of Arc," I admitted, remembering that it was due in a week. "Let me ask my mom and see if she'll bring me over," I offered, setting down my iPhone and calling down to my mom from the top of the stairs. "Mom, can you take me to a friend from school's house to work on an American History project?" I shouted down to her.

"Let me get your brother laid down for a nap, and then I'll take you. Your father will stay here with Vincent," she offered. I hurried back to my room and told Andy I'd be coming soon. He gave me some simple directions to his house and I wrote them down on a sticky note for my mom.

I hurriedly changed into jeans and a clean top. I ran a brush through my hair and applied a thin coat of lip gloss. I puckered my lips in the mirror. I'd never been so excited about doing school work on a weekend before!

Chapter Twenty-Six

Although Andy's family's luxury home looked similar to mine, it was located on a private lot surrounded by birch trees. "What is this friend from school's name again?" my mom asked, pulling into the neatly paved driveway in her Camry.

"Andy," I said, trying not to smile. I opened up my passenger side door and stepped out into the muggy heat. It was September, and way too hot for this time of year in Harrow.

My mother rolled down her window, one of those outdated kind you have to turn with a crank. "Is Andy's mother or father home?" she asked dubiously, sticking her head out the window and eyeballing the house in front of her.

"Yes, of course, Mom. We're just working on a Joan of Arc project," I promised.

By this time next year, I would hopefully have my own car and driver's license. Until then, I needed to appease my mom. "There's nothing to worry about, Mom."

I could tell by her tight smile that she trusted me, despite her concerns. She always had.

"I'll pick you up in…"she leaned in to look at the clock on her dash, "two hours."

I nodded and gave her a little wave, climbing the steps to the front door.

I was nervous as I pressed my finger firmly to the glowing doorbell. A tall, handsome woman with red hair that matched Andy's opened the door with a smile. My mother was waiting to make sure that I entered safely, and Andy's mom waved out to her, signaling that it was okay for her to leave. I waved goodbye to her as well.

"Hi, there! I'm Andy's mom, Elly," she greeted me, standing aside to let me into a fancy, wood-paneled foyer. Sitting on a tan leather sofa in a substantially sized, sunken living room, was Andy. Thick reference books were stacked on a glass coffee table in front of him. He smiled at me sheepishly, then stood up, wringing his hands nervously. "I'll leave you two to your studies." Elly gave us a little wave. She left the room, her heels clicking against the hard maple floors.

"Your mom seems nice. Is it just you and her who live here?" I sat down beside him on the sofa.

"My grandma comes to stay with us often. And my brother Cameron did live here but he just left for college this year. He's studying psychology at Butler." He glanced up at a silver-framed photo of an older redheaded boy on the fireplace mantle in front of us. It was obviously a picture of Cameron. His eyes also briefly scanned another picture—a man in a military uniform who was obviously his father. It was plain to see that he missed both his father and brother.

"Psychology? That's neat, because my mom is a therapist." My comment seemed to distract him, which is what I'd been hoping for.

"Really? That's a cool coincidence. Does she ever try to psychoanalyze you?" he asked, a serious expression on his face. I couldn't help but laugh. "No. At least I don't think she does..." I giggled.

A big furry Persian cat leapt on my lap, startling me. Andy tried to shoo her away. "Oh, it's okay. I love cats," I said, stroking its silky fur.

Talking to Andy came easy, and that's how it went for the next two hours...we talked about his father, who was stationed in Afghanistan, and I told him about my father's work as a radio engineer. Although it felt like I was talking with a friend, it was different somehow, unlike any relationship I'd had. It felt natural, the words flowing out with ease. He told me about all of the places he'd lived, moving around so much due to his father's work in the service.

By the time the text alert chimed on my iPhone with my mom's message saying she was there to pick me up, I realized that we hadn't gotten any work done on our Joan of Arc project.

"Oh, no! I can't believe it's time to go already!" I jumped up hastily, shoving a handful of notebooks and folders into my bag.

"It's okay, Dakota. We still have all week to finish it. Maybe we can try to get some work done again tomorrow?" he suggested hopefully. At the mention of tomorrow, I realized that it was almost Monday and time to find out if I'd made the squad.

"Okay. Let's try again tomorrow night. If it's okay with my mom," I said, walking toward the door. He followed, walking me out to my mom's car like a gentleman. Before I could even introduce him, he stuck his hand through the open passenger door and shook my mom's hand. Boy, he was turning out to be quite the charmer!

"I'm Andy. I have American History with Dakota. Thanks for letting her come over," he said politely. My mother was the queen of polite introductions and she seemed to be enjoying this moment.

On the ride home, she was mostly quiet, but smiling. As we approached our street, she said, "He seems perfect for you, Dakota." Having conversations with my mom about boys was slightly embarrassing, so I looked away, my cheeks heating up. But I couldn't help smiling as I stared out the window, watching the rows of houses fly by. I had to agree with my mother. *Andy does seem pretty perfect*, I thought dreamily.

Chapter Twenty-Seven

The Sociopath

I stuffed notebooks and gym wear inside my backpack, all the while balancing a can of Red Bull in my right hand. I needed to hurry, or else I'd be late for first period. Tossing my drink in the trash can by my bed, I quickly tied my shoes and stared at my reflection in the spotted up full length mirror.

"Today is the day."

I opened the closet door and removed the gun. Mossberg 500, that's what it was called. There was a heat shield over the barrel, with a pistol grip instead of a buttstock. It held eight shells, nine if you counted the one in the chamber…

A fine piece of American artillery that had belonged to my grandfather. Now it was mine.

I could hear the hiss of the bus's air brakes…it was only a few stops away.

Quickly, I slid the Mossberg into my backpack.

It was barely short enough to fit, but I just managed to get the zippers closed around it as I heard the bus screech to a halt outside. I took off running down the steps.

Today is the day.

Chapter Twenty-Eight

Dakota

When I opened my eyes, I knew that *the* day had arrived. Sunlight streamed through the gap in my curtains, illuminating my entire bedroom. A narrow beam of dust particles floated above my bed. Just like I always did when I was little, I reached up and tried to grab it.

Today was the day when the names of the new varsity squad members would be announced. I couldn't wait! I threw the covers off and started getting ready for school. I wasn't much of a morning person, and even if I had been, I wasn't one of those girls who took a long time getting ready. I pulled on a pair of stretchy leggings with shiny star patterns and topped it off with a tank top and loose fitting tee. I slipped on a pair of ballet flats, tied my hair in a perky bun, brushed my teeth, and applied a light coat of lip gloss.

"You look beautiful," my mother said as I came galloping down the steps, taking two at a time. There was this tiny electric buzz surrounding me; I was so excited! This was going to be a day I'd never forget.

My mom was feeding Vincent in a highchair, and I leaned down to give him a kiss. His lips were slobbery and stained with juice, but I didn't care. He was starting to develop a little personality all of his own and he grinned up at me, shaking his little fists in the air. "I'm excited too, little man." I smiled at him happily.

"Eggs and bacon on the stove," my mom offered, but I already knew that based on the rich, smoky aroma filling the air. I rarely saw my dad anymore, as he usually left for work before I got up and worked until late at night at the radio station. *I miss him*, I realized, chewing on a bacon strip thoughtfully. *At least he's not stationed far away in a foreign country like Andy's dad*, I reminded myself, thinking about our conversation yesterday.

"I can't eat anymore. My stomach's in knots. I think I'll just grab a banana to go," I told my mom, digging one out of the fruit bowl on the granite counter. Now that my mom had her own private practice, she could set her own hours by scheduling appointments with her individual clients. She used to work all the time like my dad, but she trimmed down her workload when Vincent was born.

"Do you have to work today?"

"Yes. Melody's going to watch your brother while I go into the office for a few hours this afternoon." Melody was our neighbor on the other side, and she's a huge help to my mom.

"If I make the team, I'll have to stay after school to get fitted for my uniform. But if not..."

"Stay positive, sweetheart," she interrupted me. "I have a good feeling you're going to make the team. I'm sorry, honey, but you might have to wait around for a bit after your fitting. Text me on my iPhone as soon as you find out if you make it, that way I can arrange my appointments and come get you from school as soon as I finish at the office." She offered an unwanted spoonful of scrambled eggs to Vincent. He pushed the eggs away playfully, spilling some on the floor.

I knew that I should have told my mom sooner about possibly having to stay after school, and I felt bad for always interfering with a career she used to love. "Don't worry about it, Mom. Sydney's mom already said she can bring me home tonight," I lied.

"Okay, wonderful! Good luck today, honey," she said, giving me a hug and kiss on top of my head.

I swung my backpack over my shoulder and headed out to the bus stop. I made it out there just in time to see the taillights of Ronnie's Trans Am turning the corner at the end of the street. *No more walking for Amanda*, I thought glumly.

But then she came running outside, both of us barely reaching the bus on time...

Chapter Twenty-Nine

When I took a seat in Biology, I realized that I had absolutely no idea when Coach Davis would make her announcement today. It could be minutes away, or hours. It could even be at the end of the day. *This wait is tortuous!* I thought impatiently.

There were no announcements during Biology, or throughout my Pre-Algebra class. I was honestly starting to think that it was not going to be until the end of the day, after all. When I got to American History, I was grateful because I knew that Andy would keep me occupied. Our teacher gave us time to work on our group projects, which was good because we hadn't started ours yet.

As soon as he and I took seats in the back to start working on it, I heard the unmistakable click of the intercom system overhead. "Attention please, students! I have an important announcement to make! This is Principal Barlow. I have Coach Davis sitting next to me and she's going to make a quick announcement regarding cheerleading tryouts."

Without realizing it, I reached across the desk and took Andy's hand in mine. My heart and stomach were fluttering like crazy!

"Good morning, students!" Coach Davis said brightly, and I could hear her shuffling papers noisily overhead.

"The six girls who made the team are...Brittani Barlow, Dakota Densford, Tally Johannsen, Amanda Loxx, Genevieve McDermott, and Monika Rutherford." At the sound of my name, I could finally breathe again. *I made it!* I fought the urge to jump up and start squealing.

Coach Davis continued, "Additionally, I have decided to select *two* alternate squad members. These two girls will practice with the team so they'll know the cheers, but they are not required to stay after school for the fitting today. The primary alternate is Sydney Hargreaves. The secondary alternate is Ashleigh Westerfield. Congratulations, girls! I will see the six squad members after school to get your uniforms and pompoms!"

At the end of her announcement, I slipped my iPhone out of my bag, and although I was not supposed to use it during class per school rules, I sent a quick text to my mom. It simply said:

I did it!

I knew she would know exactly what I meant. Andy patted me on the back and several other classmates congratulated me as well. I was so happy! It was a dream come true!

Chapter Thirty

The rest of the day breezed by, my stomach swirling in excitement. Ever since I learned that I made the squad, I'd been flying high on pure exhilaration. I was happy that the two former squad members, Monika and Tally, made the team for their senior year. I was also pleased that Amanda made the squad, even if she still wasn't talking to me. I wasn't thrilled about being on a team with Genevieve and Brittani, but I was so content with making it myself that I didn't really care about the two of them right now.

Amanda passed me in the lunch room as I was carrying my tray over to sit with Andy. Even though I was pretty sure she was still mad at me, I said, "Congratulations!" She smiled slightly and said, "You too, Dakota."

I was shocked that Sydney and Ashleigh were chosen as alternates instead of team members. I might have been pissed off at Sydney, but I knew how much she wanted to make it. Even though being an alternate was better than not making it at all, I knew she'd be heartbroken. Ashleigh was chosen as a second alternate. She'd tried out unsuccessfully the past two years, and I'd thought for sure Coach Davis would let her join the team this time. But remembering her mistakes at tryouts, I realized that it did make sense. I still felt bad for her.

I looked around for Sydney all day, but never saw her. I was starting to wonder if she was out sick from school today. I did, however, see Ashleigh in between my last two classes while I was standing at my locker. I expected her to look upset about being chosen as an alternate, but it was quite the contrary. She seemed to be glowing.

"Good job at making the team, Dakota!" she said sweetly, leaning against the locker beside me while I switched out text books. I wasn't sure what to say back to her, but then finally I said, "I wish you would have made it too. But I'm glad you were chosen as an alternate, Ashleigh."

"After two years of not making the squad, I'm just happy I get to be a part of it this year. I'll get to come to games and practice with you guys, and I may even get to fill in sometimes!" she said ecstatically. I was astounded and impressed by her positive outlook. I could only hope that Sydney shared her views when it came to being an alternate.

Genevieve's pal, Mariella, didn't make the team at all, and I wasn't surprised by the dirty look she gave me when I passed by her later in the day. I noticed that she was hanging out by Tasha's locker. I wouldn't have been surprised to see those two teaming up now since they didn't make the team. I decided not to worry about it. Today was a happy day and I planned on enjoying every minute of it! I couldn't wait to check out my uniform and pompoms after school.

Chapter Thirty-One

At the end of the day, I followed Brittani Barlow to the gymnasium for our meeting with Coach Davis. I hadn't planned on walking with her, but she followed me out of Study Hall, leaving me no choice.

"I'm so excited about making the team! Aren't you?" She was beaming from ear to ear.

"I still haven't forgotten what you did to get on the team, Brittani. If you hadn't intentionally dropped Teresa, you may not have made it." I narrowed my eyes at her.

Normally, I wouldn't be so harsh, but I was not going to be friends with someone who could do something so evil to someone else. "It's *you*, not me, who wouldn't have made the team if I hadn't done what I did. You should be *thanking* me, Dakota," she remarked, pushing past me and skipping on over to the entrance of the gym.

Forgetting about Brittani's insanity, I headed

into the gym. Coach Davis was already waiting for us. When everyone arrived, she used a measuring tape to calculate our body measurements, and she also had each of us write down our shoe size. She scribbled down our sizes speedily, moving from one of us to the other.

"Okay, girls! Some of you will have to wait for your uniforms to be altered a bit to suit your size, but some of you can take yours home today. She unzipped a large black bag that, oddly enough, resembled one of those bags they put dead people in on TV. It was filled with a stack of crisp red and gold uniforms. The top of the uniform was a half-top with the word **'Dragons'** scrawled across the chest for our team mascot. The bottom was a short, pleated skirt. They were the most awesome uniforms I'd ever seen, and I couldn't wait to try mine on!

Coach Davis also had a stack of bodysuits to wear under the uniform top and a bag filled to the brim with pompoms. Considering the fact that I was a little chunky and short, I'd assumed that I'd definitely have to wait for alterations to my uniform. I was pleasantly surprised when she called my name first, and handed me my uniform, bodysuit, and pompoms to take home with me.

As much as I wanted to control my emotions, I couldn't wipe the smile from my face as I accepted my items and returned to the bleachers with the other team members. Tally and Brittani received their uniforms, but the other girls only got pompoms and body suits.

"Practice will begin tomorrow after school. Our

first game of the season is next week, so we must get ready. Tomorrow, I'll give each of you a game and practice schedule so you'll know the dates and times for both.

"Also, after careful consideration, I have decided that Brittani and Amanda will be the main bases for our stunts. Monika and Genevieve, since you're both the tallest on the team, you will bring up the rear. Tally, you're our best tumbler, so you will stay in the front and tumble during most of the lifts. And for the top of the stunts, Dakota is the shortest, so she will be our designated flyer."

Never in a million years could I have imagined that I'd get to be the one on top of the stunts. It was all so much to take in, and almost hard to believe. I had to pinch myself to make sure the moment was real.

Chapter Thirty-Two

Lying to my mother this morning wasn't a good idea. Not only did I have to walk several miles to get home now, but I had to walk in the rain. Without an umbrella. And with a brand new cheerleading uniform, body suit, and pompoms in tow. I'd told my mom I was riding with Sydney even though that was a lie. However, if Sydney really were here I would ask her mom to take me home in a heartbeat. Unfortunately, she didn't make the team, so that wasn't even an option.

I looked down at my awesome new cheerleading gear. I couldn't wait to get home and try it all on in my bedroom. And I couldn't wait to show my mom!

The last thing I wanted or needed to do was damage my brand new uniform and the rest of my stuff by taking it out in the rain.

The hallways of the school were eerily deserted. I used the girls' restroom, listening intently for the psycho-breather, and then paced around the front entranceway, hoping the rain would die down a bit. It didn't.

From the deserted entranceway, I watched Ronnie and Amanda pulling away in his Trans Am. I didn't miss Ronnie, but I *did* miss having Amanda as my friend. *I guess my mom was right after all*, I thought drearily. I waited around for a few more minutes, unsure what to do. It wasn't getting wet that I worried about; it was the idea of tearing up my uniform.

I pulled out my iPhone, and dialed the number to my mom's office. I recognized the voice of the girl who answered. It was Phoebe, my mom's faithful secretary. "Hey, it's Dakota. Is my mom available?" I tried to hide the impatience in my voice.

"She's in session with a client right now. Her **'Do Not Disturb'** sign is on the door, but if it's important, sweetheart, I'll be more than happy to interrupt her."

"No, that's okay. Just tell her I'll see her at home tonight. Bye." I hung up before I let her talk me into it.

I suddenly realized that I could simply just leave my uniform stuff in my locker until tomorrow. I wanted more than anything to take it home with me, but it was worth waiting so I didn't damage it. I jogged back down the hallway, stuffed it all inside my locker, and headed out into the gloomy weather, holding a thin windbreaker over my head to shield the rain.

Chapter Thirty-Three

Running through a downpour, I was hit with a brilliant idea. Andy only lived a few blocks from school, and we'd discussed the possibility of getting together to work on Joan of Arc today. *Would he think it was weird if I just showed up?* I wondered. I could have stopped and called, but I doubted I could hear anything with this rainfall, and I didn't want to stop running.

I ran as fast as I could, feeling happy and alive despite the chill in the air. I had a guy that I liked and I actually made the varsity cheerleading team! Who could ask for anything better?

I rounded the corner of Emery Lane, and I was relieved to see his house just a few yards away. There was a sporty blue Celica parked in front of his house on the street. I stopped and bent down to catch my breath, resting my hands on my knees as I drew in deep gulps of air.

Just as I was getting ready to walk that way, the

passenger door to the Celica swung open and Andy stepped out of it. A girl stepped out of the driver's side. She was pretty, with wavy white-blonde hair and a trim figure. She walked around the side of the car, and draped her arms over his shoulders. A seductive gesture.

They stood there kissing in the rain.

This was the part when I should have run away crying, but instead, I curled my fingers into fists and let out a frustrated scream. *I'm so sick of people hurting me, and not being the people I think they are!* I thought angrily.

The sound of my scream caught their attention, and they both turned to look my way, stunned. "Dakota?" Andy called out, and he walked toward me. That's when I turned around and ran.

Rain was still falling as I made my way home, but I barely even noticed. I was thinking about Andy, Sydney, and Amanda. I was thinking about what Brittani did and how I didn't tell anyone about it. I couldn't stop the tears from falling down my cheeks even if I wanted to. I let the water from my tears and the rain flow freely down my face as I kept moving.

A pair of headlights glowed from behind me, and I heard a car screech to a halt. I turned around to see Mom's Camry, and I'd never been so relieved to see my mother and take a ride with her. She didn't ask any questions. She just patted my leg and drove me home.

"Thanks, Mom," I told her, wiping my face with the back of my hand. "How did you know that I needed a ride?" I finally asked.

"After Phoebe told me you called, and I couldn't reach you on your phone, I just had a feeling that I should come," she explained, softly. *Leave it to my mom to be the only one in the world who understands me.*

She fixed my favorite: Gorgonzola pasta. I told her everything over dinner, the good parts of the day and the bad. She listened sympathetically and encouraged me to focus on my cheerleading practice, and let the other stuff work itself out. All I could do was try.

Chapter Thirty-Four

The Sociopath

Yesterday was not *the* day. I carried the gun from class to class, waiting for just the right moment…but it never came. Although the element of surprise is exciting, I think I'll torture my sheep a little bit…toy with their minds.

I opened the closet. Stared at the gun.

I considered packing it again, but instead I went to the fridge. My specimen was still intact. Well, I don't know if *intact* is the right choice of words…

I lifted the plastic container, the cat's fluids sloshing around inside. Carefully, I slid the container inside my backpack.

Today's going to be fun.

Chapter Thirty-Five

Dakota

My mother had this uncanny ability to cheer me up with only a few simple words. Despite last night's disappointment, I woke up in a better mood. Andy was not my boyfriend, and if he wanted to date someone else that was his business. I honestly had no idea who that girl was he was hanging out with, but I was not going to waste my time worrying about it today. I was going to focus on what was most important to me: Cheerleading.

Yanking a pale pink, knee-length dress that I'd never worn before off its hanger, I pulled it down over my head. I slid on a pair of white Keds and dabbed some pink lipstick on to match my dress.

Amanda was standing at the bus stop, actually looking at me as though she wanted to talk. "Are you okay?" she asked, giving me a sympathetic look. I realized then that she must have been talking about what happened with Andy, but I had no idea how she could know.

"What do you mean?" I asked, sounding a little defensive.

"Well, I was sitting outside under the awning when you came home with your mom last night. You were soaking wet and crying. I was just wondering if you're all right." She carefully adjusted her bag on her shoulder. "I know we haven't been talking, but I still care about your well-being."

"I'm okay now. There was this boy I thought I liked, but as it turns out, he didn't feel the same way about me." I looked anxiously up the street for the bus to arrive.

"I'm sorry, Dakota." She searched my eyes, waiting for more of the story.

"I'm sorry too. And I would never be a part of what those girls did to your grandma's house and I'd never write a note like that, I swear. I did tell Sydney that you and Ronnie were kissing outside, and I'm sorry for that. I wasn't trying to be malicious when I told her, and I never expected Sydney to go behind my back and cause so much trouble with those other girls."

"I know you didn't do it. And I'm sorry about dating your ex. It's just…he's the first boy that's paid any attention to me since I moved to Harrow Hill, and I jumped on the opportunity to have a boyfriend. I can't help who I like, but I do want to be friends again. I'm so happy we both made the team. Can we be friends again, please?" she asked hopefully.

"Of course." I smiled and leaned forward to give her a hug. "Did you rehearse that whole spiel ahead of time?" I teased.

"Only a hundred times…" she admitted, smiling back. I realized then how much I'd really missed having her around to talk to.

"Are you ready for our first real practice tonight?" I raised my eyebrows in challenge.

"As ready as I'm going to be! Are you so excited about being the flyer?"

"I'm excited, but also nervous. I've never been on the top of a stunt before," I admitted. "I always thought I was too chubby to be the girl on top." I stared down at my Keds.

"You are perfect, Dakota!" Amanda said, nudging me playfully.

"Thanks. And thanks for making up with me," I said, happy to have my friend back. I was glad that she'd be one of the people lifting me in the stunts because I trusted her completely.

It suddenly dawned on me who the other base was: Brittani. After what she did to Teresa, how could I trust her not to do the same to me? *Now I really do have a reason to be nervous when it comes to being the flyer!* I realized.

Amanda and I talked about cheerleading the whole way to school. When we got there, I made a beeline for my locker, eager to catch a glimpse of my new uniform again. I turned the dial back and forth, remembering the combination with ease now that I'd opened it so many times. I swung open the thin metal door, and immediately screamed in horror. My uniform, body suit, and pompoms had been ripped to shreds.

Chapter Thirty-Six

I wish I could say that I played it cool, but in truth, I bawled like a baby right there in the hall. Amanda was only a few paces away, and she ran to my side, wrapping her arms around me. "What is it, Dakota?" she asked, her voice trembling with fear. I pointed at the locker and she looked for herself.

I couldn't look again. People in the hallway were forming a crowd, excited to see what all of the commotion was about. *Could this get any worse*? I wondered, trying to wipe the tears off my face with the back of my hand.

I couldn't believe it. *Why would somebody do this to me?* "It looks like someone sliced through it with a knife, and there's red sticky stuff all over the pompoms." Amanda winced.

"Hey, it looks like blood!" a sophomore boy yelled, causing laughter to erupt among several other students. "I think someone is out to get you," a strange redheaded boy said behind me. Another round of sarcastic "oooooh" noises. I wanted to punch all of their lights out.

I looked around at my classmates. Some of them I knew, but most of them I didn't. Who would do this to me? It was obviously someone who didn't want me on the squad. *Probably someone who didn't make it themselves*, I realized.

A wall of kids surrounded me, but I could still see Tasha and Mariella toward the back of the crowd. They both looked satisfied, wearing ugly, spiteful smirks on their faces. I stared at them defiantly. *Genevieve and Sydney might be involved as well*, I considered. I suddenly remembered Coach Davis's voice, telling us that there were only six sets of uniforms. Without a uniform, how was I going to cheer?

I might have to sit on the sidelines all season, I realized miserably. *This could be the end of my dream of being a varsity cheerleader...*

Chapter Thirty-Seven

The first period bell rang, causing the gawkers to scatter in different directions. *Sort of like cockroaches*, I thought, feeling disgusted. Amanda remained at my side. “Go on to class, I’ll take care of this.” I slammed shut the locker with its hideous contents.

“Are you sure? What are you going to do?” she asked, placing a comforting hand on my shoulder.

“I’m going to see Coach Davis.”

I might get in trouble for not showing up to Biology, but I was past the point of caring. I walked down the east end hallway, locating the door to Coach Davis’s English class. The door was closed, but I could see her through a pane of glass. She was standing up, teaching a room full of students. I didn’t know how she’d react about my uniform. *She might even blame me because I left it in my locker*, I considered, feeling apprehensive. I raised my fist and knocked anyway.

When Coach Davis opened the door, she could immediately tell something was wrong. She stuck her head back inside the classroom, told her students to read the next section of *Beowulf*, and followed me out to the hall. "What happened, Dakota? Are you okay?" She was wearing a look of concern on her face.

I blurted out everything. I told her about lying to my mother about having a ride home after the fitting, about putting my uniform in the locker to keep it from getting damaged in the rain, and finding it this morning torn to bits. "I'm sorry, Coach. If you want to kick me off the team, I'll understand." Tears were once again streaming down my face.

"Dakota, I would prefer that you didn't keep your uniform in your locker in the future, but this ultimately was not your fault. Whoever did this to you was obviously jealous about you making the team. I'll talk to Principal Barlow and have her order you a brand new uniform. I will have to get it ordered today so it'll be here in time for game night. Our first night is in less than a week, but I'll pull some strings with the company that makes our uniforms and have UPS ship it for us so it will get here faster."

I let out a whoosh of breath and hugged Coach tightly. She looked a little surprised by my embrace. I was so relieved that I felt like kissing her! "Thank you so much, Coach Davis! And I promise this will never happen again!"

"Go to class. I'll have a janitor clean out your locker and we'll also try to get to the bottom of who did this. Whoever it was…they might be out to get not only you, but everyone else on the squad," she warned.

Chapter Thirty-Eight

After the morning I'd had, I wasn't in the mood for dealing with Andy. But he was waiting for me in third period, just like I suspected he would be. "I heard about what happened. Are you okay?" He reached out, touching my shoulder gently. I brushed him off.

"I'm fine, really. Coach Davis is ordering a new uniform," I assured him, sitting down nonchalantly at my desk.

"About last night…" he started to say, taking a seat at the desk in front of me. I put up a palm to stop him.

"You don't owe me any explanations, Andy. I'm not your girlfriend. In fact, we barely even know each other. We were just randomly paired together to do a stupid history project." I refused to look up, afraid to meet his eyes. I could feel a huge lump forming in the back of my throat.

"I thought we had something more and I know

you felt the same way, Dakota. The girl that was at my house…her name is Winter Addams. We used to go out when I lived in Salem. Her dad is in the service too. She's moving to Hawaii in a few days, and I'll never see her again. She came to tell me goodbye. I didn't want to hurt her feelings, so I let her kiss me."

"Oh, give me a break," I muttered, pulling a notebook and pen out of my backpack. Our history teacher, Mr. Schwartz, entered the room and commanded us to be quiet.

"It's true," Andy hissed, then turned around in his seat to face the front of the room. I wanted to believe him, I really did. But I didn't want to get my heart broken, and I had other things to worry about.

Chapter Thirty-Nine

After going through the lunch line, I was thankful to see Amanda saving me a seat. I sat down beside her with my grilled cheese sandwich and tomato basil soup. The red coloring of the soup reminded me of the red paint covering my pompoms. Suddenly, I didn't feel hungry anymore.

"Are you doing okay?" Amanda asked softly, taking a sip from her own bowl of soup. I was getting sick of hearing people ask me that question.

"I'm fine. Coach Davis ordered me new gear," I repeated flatly.

"I've been thinking…do you think the same person or persons that wrote that note and egged my grandma's house also tore up your stuff?" It was a good question, and one that I'd already considered.

"I was watching out the window that night, remember? I'm pretty sure it was Tasha, Genevieve, and Mariella wearing those masks. I think Genevieve instigated that whole event because she was jealous about you dating Ronnie. I guess they could have done this to me too. From the looks of things, Tasha and Mariella want nothing to do with Genevieve or Tally now that they made the cheerleading squad." I pointed over at Genevieve and Tally, who were sitting by themselves today.

"It would've taken only one person to tear up the stuff in my locker, and I wouldn't put it past any of them," I added, with a deep sigh. I took a small bite of my sandwich. At this point, I didn't care who did it as long as it never happened again. I would never, ever have to find out because I didn't plan on leaving my uniform at school anymore.

"Could *she* have done it?" Amanda pointed across the lunchroom. I followed her line of vision. She was talking about Sydney. "She had a reason for wanting to tear up that uniform. She didn't make the team, and she's been jealous of our friendship ever since school started," Amanda reminded me, making a whole lot of sense.

I didn't want to believe that Sydney could be capable of doing that to me. As I sat there, staring at my old best friend, she looked up as though she could feel my glare. We locked eyes. She smiled at me, but the smile was strange, almost self-satisfactory. *Would Sydney really do that me?*

"How did they know your locker combination, anyway?" Amanda asked out of the blue, making my blood run cold. There was only one person who had ever known my locker combination. Two weeks before school started, Sydney and I came up to school together to do a tour of our classes and check out our lockers. We both practiced opening them together multiple times. She helped me open mine a few times, so it was very possible that she memorized the combination. I didn't want to accept this possible truth, but I was starting to think that it really could be her. I couldn't help feeling devastated.

Chapter Forty

"Dakota, are you okay?" Brittani asked, before I could even take a seat in Study Hall. I took a deep breath and exhaled.

"I'm okay. Thanks for asking."

"What are you going to do about the uniform?" She frowned worriedly.

"Coach Davis is getting me a new one," I answered dully, sick of this line of questioning.

"My mother keeps a binder in her office with everyone's locker combinations in it. In case someone forgets their combo and needs her to open it for them, you know? Anyone could have stolen that book, and used it to break into your locker," she explained, perfectly composed.

I sat there, stunned.

"Did *you* break into my locker, Brittani?" I clenched my teeth together, seething.

"Me? Oh, of course not. I'm just telling you a simple observation I've made. I have no idea why someone would do that to you, honestly. And I'd never do something so awful…"

So, she won't tear up a stupid uniform, but she'll let somebody break a leg? What a psycho!

I nodded slowly. Surely she wouldn't be stupid enough to tell me about the binder if she was the one who did it. I unzipped my backpack and took out my Joan of Arc book that I'd borrowed from the school library. I planned on doing most of the project on my own, that way I didn't have to be alone with Andy anymore. Even if that Winter chick was his ex and moving far away, he wouldn't have kissed her if he really liked me. Simple as that.

A shrill cry interjected my thoughts. Brittani was standing up beside her desk, screaming. In an instant, students were gathering all around her, and Mrs. Bartlett was trying to push her way through the crowd to make sure Brittani was okay.

I hesitantly made my way over too, trying to catch a glimpse of what was happening. Brittani was pointing down at her open gym bag, a hand covering her mouth in horror.

That's when I saw what she was looking at. I winced, covering my own nose with my hands.

There appeared to be a bloody, hairy mass inside of her bag. It smelled. *How did we not notice that smell before?*

I instantly saw my answer. Surrounding the bloody hairball were tiny air freshener trees…someone obviously wanted to mask the smell for as long as possible.

"What is it?" I heard someone shout. Other students were backing up, and one girl appeared to be crying. I was too afraid to step closer.

Suddenly, someone shouted, "It's a dead kitten!"

Several people shouted, "Ewww!" Everyone started backing away from it.

I could hear sounds of someone gagging near the back of the room.

Mrs. Bartlett used the two-way radio on her hip to call for Principal Barlow. Brittani was still staring down at the bag, her face as hard as stone. I thought about the goofy leotard she had on last week at tryouts, the one with the cute little kittens on the front. I thought about my shredded uniform. I couldn't help wondering if somebody had it out for all of the girls who made the team, just like Coach Davis predicted.

Chapter Forty-One

I walked with Brittani to cheer practice. Despite our differences, I felt sorry for her. She was in a trancelike state, and I was pretty sure she was traumatized. I gave her a tank top and gym shorts to wear, since hers were in the gym bag with the bloody cat.

Brittani's mother, Principal Barlow, had rushed to the scene in Mrs. Bartlett's room. She'd used a pair of plastic gloves to carry the bag to her office. Supposedly, she had plans to contact the police.

"When do you suppose someone put the kitten into your bag?" I asked Brittani hesitantly. She winced at the word "kitten." Swallowing hard, she said, "I took my gym bag to P.E. fourth period. I got my tennis shoes out of it and everything was fine then. I left it in the locker room while we were outside playing tennis. I left the shoes on when I went to my next class because I knew I'd need to keep them on for practice today. The next time I opened the bag, I found…well, you know…"

She began sobbing again. For someone who seemed to care so little about the people around her, she sure was upset over this cat. I didn't blame her. The sight of it had been terrible, and I wondered if I'd ever be able to erase it from my mind. That messy clump of fur, with its twisted, bloody limbs…and the worst part of all—that smell. I shuddered.

"Did you see anyone hanging around your bag or messing with your stuff?" I scratched my head. I just couldn't figure out how someone could carry around a dead cat all day and then stick it in Brittani's gym bag without anyone seeing it. Brittani shook her head no.

"Anybody could have done it while I was outside. I left the bag right out in the open on the locker room floor."

Entering the gym, we were a few minutes late because of the whole ordeal, but Principal Barlow had already informed Coach Davis about the incident. Amanda, Genevieve, Monika, and Tally were sitting on the hard, wooden gym floor in front of Coach Davis. Sydney and Ashleigh were there too; since they're the alternates, they had to attend some practices in order to familiarize themselves with the cheers, in case they had to fill in.

"Come in, girls. Come sit down with us. I want to make an announcement." Coach Davis motioned for us to come over. Brittani and I took a seat on the floor with the others. "Although learning our routines for next Tuesday's game is very important, my number one concern is your safety." She looked down at each and every one of us, her arms tightly crossed over her chest.

"This morning someone broke into Dakota's locker. They tore up her uniform and pompoms. Brittani found a dead kitten in her gym bag. The police are down in Principal Barlow's office right now. Apparently, upon closer inspection, they have determined that someone killed the cat with a knife. It was perhaps the same knife used to tear up Dakota's cheerleading items. They also believe that the red substance on your pompoms is blood that came from the cat," she said grimly, looking at me with a pained expression.

My stomach flip flopped, and for a moment, I thought I might get sick right there on the gym floor. I squeezed my eyes shut, willing the image to leave my mind.

"The thought of someone from this school doing these things…it's very unsettling, to say the least. It's probably just a jealous prank, but I want all of you to be extra careful. Travel in pairs, and no walking home from school alone," she added, looking at me specifically. We all nodded in agreement.

"Coach Davis?" Monika called out abruptly from where she was sitting on the floor. Monika and Tally were looking back and forth at each other nervously. "Someone slashed mine and Tally's car tires today. We saw that both of us had a flat tire when we went out to our cars to get our gym bags before practice. Do you think it's the same person?" Her voice trembled slightly.

Coach Davis nodded. "I do. And I'm going to let

Principal Barlow know immediately so the police can take a look at your vehicles," she said sternly, picking up her two-way radio. She turned her back to us and walked several paces away before barking into the radio at Principal Barlow.

We all looked back and forth at each other anxiously as we listened to her relay the news of Monika and Tally's incident. *A knife…used to slash tires, rip my cheer gear, and…kill a cat*, I thought gravely.

When she was done, Coach Davis clapped her hands together. "Let's start practicing!"

We jumped to our feet. I wasn't sure how capable we'd be when it came to learning cheers. I was totally freaked out and more certain than ever that someone was trying to harm the new Harrow High squad members.

Chapter Forty-Two

My mom was waiting for me when I came out of practice. Seeing her was like a breath of fresh air after an emotionally stifling day.

"Is Ronnie coming to pick you up?" I asked Amanda, who was looking up and down the parking lot for his Trans Am.

"He said he might be running late," she replied warily.

"Why don't you just text him and tell him my mom will bring you home? I don't want you to wait here alone. Remember what Coach Davis told us about traveling in pairs…" My voice was edged with concern.

Our relationship had been rocky lately, but I was concerned for Amanda's well-being and wouldn't take no for an answer. "Okay," she finally agreed, texting on her cell phone to Ronnie as she climbed into my mom's backseat. My little brother was in the back today too, so I climbed up front with my mom.

"Where's your uniform?" I knew she could already sense my distress. I told her what happened. I also told her about Monika and Tally's slashed tires, and the disgusting discovery in Brittani's bag.

"It sounds like you might be dealing with a sociopath." Her lips tightened, the way they always did when she was worried.

"What's a sociopath?" Amanda asked fearfully, leaning forward from her seat in the back.

"Someone who lacks the ability to feel remorse. They are manipulative and enjoy hurting others. They also often enjoy torturing animals."

Amanda and I looked at each other, worried. My mom was one of the most intelligent women I knew, but I hoped like hell she was wrong. If she *was* right, then we could be in serious danger.

Chapter Forty-Three

The next day was Wednesday, and I expected the sociopath to strike again. But the day went on without a hitch. I worked on my history project with Andy in class, but I was careful to stay on topic. He tried to joke around and be playful, but I did my best not to react to his charm.

I passed my oral Spanish test and avoided Sydney like the plague in Phys Ed. I think she was avoiding me too. At the sound of the final bell, I felt relief. An entire day with no incidents.

I headed to the gym for practice, astonished to see approximately ten boys running up and down the court playing a game of scrimmage. A few of them were freshman boys that I recognized. Ronnie and Andy were guarding each other. My stomach fluttered awkwardly at the sight of them both.

"I didn't know the boys were practicing in here today." Coach Davis clucked her tongue, obviously irritated. Tally was standing beside me too, and we exchanged knowing looks. There was a rumor going around that Coach Davis used to date the basketball coach, Coach Purnell, in high school. I wasn't sure if there was any truth to the rumor, but based on the way she was glaring across the court at him, I thought it might be possible.

Coach Davis strolled across the court boldly, cutting straight through the ongoing game, and heated words were exchanged between her and Coach Purnell. He looked almost intimidated. I couldn't contain a small snort of laughter. After their exchange, Coach Purnell and the boys moved to one side of the court, giving us plenty of room to practice on the other side.

Yesterday we learned six new cheers, and today we learned five more. The cheers were short and simple to learn. The halftime cheer, however, was more complex and involved me doing a standing back tuck, and being lifted into an extension prep.

After learning the sideline chants, it was time to practice the stunt. "Don't you dare drop me on purpose," I snarled at Brittani.

"I won't!" she squeaked, looking surprised by my concern. It wasn't like she hadn't done it before, right? I rolled my eyes at her and got in position to step into the lift.

"One, two, down, up," the bases called out in unison, dipping down as I stepped onto their hands. The next thing I knew their arms were fully extended and I was up in the air.

My arms and legs felt shaky. "Remember to pretend there's a penny in your butt cheeks! Keep your butt and legs tight!" Coach Davis shouted. I did as she commanded.

"And smile up there!" I smiled out at the non-existent crowd.

However, even though there were no fans in the stands, there was a crowd watching me. Most of the boys had stopped what they were doing and they were staring at our stunt. Andy stared at me longingly, bracing a ball on his hip. I also saw Ronnie staring at me strangely.

"One, two, down, up," they said again, performing a basket toss to let me down from the lift safely.

"Great job, girls! You were terrific, Dakota," Coach Davis praised. I was absolutely exhilarated. Not only did I love being a flyer, but I was good at it too! I couldn't wait for game night, and the "sociopath" was the farthest thing from my mind…

Chapter Forty-Four

I was still flying high from yesterday's practice when I saw that the sociopath had struck again. There were dozens of white paper fliers stuck to the doors of lockers and strung out all along the hallway. There had to be hundreds of them.

As I got closer, I saw that the flier contained a black and white picture of Amanda, pasted next to a mug shot of a man. I didn't understand the meaning of them, but I knew the fliers contained something bad about my friend. I hastily walked up to the first one and started yanking them down furiously.

"It's no use. They're everywhere." Amanda stood quietly behind me. Her eyes were red-rimmed and swollen.

"The sociopath?" She nodded grimly.

We walked from locker to locker, taking fliers down on each side of the hall. But people were picking them up off the floor and staring at the ones that were still hanging. "Sounds to me like your dad got what he deserved." Tasha held up one of the papers defiantly.

Amanda tried to lunge at her, but I grabbed her around the waist and held her back with as much strength as I could muster. "You bitch! I know you did this! You're the one doing all of this!" Amanda fought against my arms.

"I wish I could take credit for it." Tasha giggled, running off down the hallway with an armful of fliers.

The bell rang and students cleared out of the hallway slowly. I didn't care about getting to class on time, or at all. I had to fix this somehow. I let go of Amanda, who was calmer now that Tasha was gone, and I bent down to pick up more fliers from the floor. That's when I really looked at the paper for the first time.

The mugshot belonged to Terrance Loxx, convicted of armed robbery and murder. Under the photos of him and Amanda was a copy of a newspaper article. I skimmed as much of it as I could, as speedily as possible, so that it wasn't obvious to Amanda that I was reading it. The article was about a man who was in a standoff with police officers. He had been shot and killed, but not before committing a murder. The man in the article was Amanda's father.

Below Amanda's picture was a question:

Like father, like daughter?

I winced. The sociopath had stooped to a new low with this act.

"This is pointless. The fliers are in the other hallways too! We can't get them all." Amanda threw up her hands in exasperation.

"What's going on?" asked a female voice from one of the classrooms. I recognized the woman as one of the sophomore math teachers.

"Can you use your walkie talkie to call for Principal Barlow? We need help getting all of these fliers removed as quickly as possible," I said, taking charge of the situation.

"It'll be okay," I told Amanda, but I wasn't so sure myself. The devastated look on her face was heartbreaking and I felt terrible for my friend.

With our arms wrapped around each other's waists, we waited for Principal Barlow to come help us.

Chapter Forty-Five

It took Principal Barlow and the janitor until almost lunchtime to track down all of the fliers and discard them. I'm sure there were still a few floating around…

Amanda was sullen as we sat at the lunch table with our Caesar salads and fruit bowls. There were several of our classmates sitting around us, but they got up and moved.

I noticed that people were staring at us. Well, not *us* per se, but Amanda. I returned their ugly stares with a few pretty ugly looks myself. I also heard a lot of whispering. Even if Amanda's dad was a criminal, that had nothing to do with her. *If anything, people should feel sorry for her because of it*, I thought crossly. My classmates' childishness was deeply upsetting.

"Hey, guys." Andy set down his tray, taking a seat across me.

"Hi," I replied, smiling at him sincerely. *The fact*

that he doesn't care what people think about him for sitting with us is another trait I love about him, I realized. I suddenly didn't feel like staying mad at him any longer.

"That lift you guys did at practice yesterday was awesome. So, how heavy does Dakota's big butt feel when you have to raise her up like that?" he asked Amanda, winking at me. She smiled back at him.

"She feels like a ton of bricks when I have to lift her over my head." Amanda nudged me, grinning.

"Hey, now!" I laughed, smiling at them both.

"Are you guys going to do that lift at halftime?" he asked. Amanda nodded.

"We're doing a routine and then the lift is at the very end," she explained, popping a grape into her mouth.

I mouthed the words 'thank you' to Andy. I was so grateful he had gotten Amanda's mind off the incident with the fliers. I watched him as he made her laugh, and had to admit that even though he hurt me, I wanted to forgive him and give him another shot.

Chapter Forty-Six

"How does someone become a sociopath, Mom?"

We were eating fettuccini Alfredo and crisp asparagus spears for dinner. My dad had gotten off early from work. When I asked the question, he looked from me to my mom, and then put his head back down toward his food.

My mom smiled at me. She was feeding little bits of noodle and asparagus to Vincent, who was sitting in his highchair happily. "There are lots of different theories, honey. There is rarely one simple cause that makes people the way they are. It's usually much more complex than that, a combination of factors…"

"Well, what do you think could possibly be *some* of the reasons?" I asked. She chewed her food thoughtfully.

"People who develop sociopathic tendencies usually come from abusive homes. Not always, but more times than not. One of the main theories is that they don't form healthy relationships with their parents at an early age, and because of that, they never learn normal empathic skills. They often come from broken homes with parents who have drug problems, or problems with the law. In other words, sociopaths often have sociopathic parents. When I told you that the other day, about how maybe you're dealing with a sociopath, I was wrong to say that. Kids your age are too young for that sort of diagnosis, honey. But you could be dealing with someone that has those sorts of traits. Does that make sense?" I nodded. It sort of did.

"So, are you ready for the big game Tuesday?" I could tell she was trying to change the subject to a more pleasant topic.

"Yes! I think we're going to do well. Coach Davis said that my uniform will be delivered on Monday. Just in time for the opening game!"

"That's great, honey," Mom said.

"I have to work, but I'll try to come to at least one of your games this season," my dad chimed in, finally joining the conversation.

"I understand, Dad. I hope you can come to one, but if not, I'll understand." I finished my last bite of noodles.

I put my plate in the sink, heading upstairs for a shower. Even though I wanted to focus on the upcoming game, my thoughts kept drifting back to my mom's words and all of the evil things that happened to us this week. Somebody obviously had it out for the cheerleaders.

If I could only figure out who was doing it, I

might be able to stop it. Before he or she did something even worse. Whoever it was, they had to be smart. They had to sneak the cat into Brittani's bag and break into my locker without anyone seeing them do it. They had to slit Monika and Tally's tires out in the parking lot without being seen as well. They also had to research all of that information about Amanda and her father.

I thought about the possible suspects. Tasha was mean as hell, but not very smart. I couldn't see her masterminding the whole thing. Sydney was smart. Scary smart. But her mom and dad were the most perfect parents ever, and when I thought about my mom's profile, of someone from a dysfunctional family, she definitely didn't fit.

A thought was taking shape in my mind, but I couldn't grasp it yet. What was it that my mom said exactly? Sociopaths often come from broken homes, with parents who have drug problems or criminal problems…and then it hit me. I only had one friend who fit that profile, and she fit it perfectly. Amanda.

Chapter Forty-Seven

I tossed and turned all night, my nightmares filled with images of dead kittens and bloody pompoms. When I opened my eyes, it was only a quarter past midnight. It felt like I'd been dreaming for hours. I closed my eyes and tried to fall back asleep, but kept thinking about Amanda.

It was an absurd idea. If she were the one doing all of this, then that meant she would have also been the person who hung up her own fliers. Why would she do that? It made no sense whatsoever.

But her dad was crazy, obviously. He had killed someone, according to the flier. I thought about the question on the flier. *Like father, like daughter?* Even if it was her, what would be her motivation? I couldn't think of any reasons for her to do it. She made the cheerleading team and she got the guy she wanted…why would she sabotage all that?

But then again, maybe she was trying to get back at us for that little prank—the egging and the note to

Grandma Mimi…

I decided it was time to do a little research of my own. I got out of bed and turned on the lamp beside my desk. My laptop was on from earlier when I'd been working on my Joan of Arc project. I pulled up the Google search menu and typed in the search words ***'Terrance Loxx'*** and ***'murder.'***" The screen immediately filled with relevant articles about Amanda's father. I skimmed through one of them and moved on to the next. I read several more after that.

Basically, Terrance Loxx was a bad apple. He grew up on the rough side of Chicago. His mother had a drug problem, and he left home as a preteen. He begged and stole for money. He was in and out of juvenile detention as a youth for petty theft charges. He graduated to the Big Leagues of crime after the age of eighteen, and served a year in Maxwell Prison for theft. At age nineteen, he went back to prison for theft. He apparently had a drug problem too, because he racked up multiple drug felonies.

At some point, in his mid-twenties, he met Bethany Alsworth. They had a baby girl together. They named her Amanda.

Her dad apparently tried to straighten up his act for a while by getting clean. But five years ago, he'd relapsed and resorted to stealing again. On a cold winter day, Terrance Loxx walked into a bank with a gun. When he realized that the teller had hit an emergency alert sensor, he shot her and five other people who were standing nearby. Two of those people were a pregnant woman and her eight-year-old son. He ran from the scene but was found a few hours later, at his girlfriend's house, clutching his ten-year-old daughter, Amanda.

He had a standoff with the police and lost. They shot him dead in the yard with his girlfriend and daughter watching.

I squeezed my eyes shut and opened them again. Amanda's dad was a bad dude. No doubt about that. Perhaps Genevieve was right when she said he got what he deserved. But my heart ached for my friend. I couldn't imagine seeing someone I loved get shot down like that, especially if that someone was my father. And witnessing something like that at such a young age…

Experiencing a trauma of that magnitude was bound to cause some mental problems. But would it cause Amanda to torture a cat or do those other crazy things? I wasn't sure. I certainly hoped I was wrong about this…

Suddenly, there was a loud tap at my window. I spun around in my computer chair, frozen with fear. There it was again. *Tap. Tap. Tap.* My bedroom window was on the second floor, so no one could possibly be standing near the window sill.

Tap. Tap. Tap. I turned on my bedroom light just as a small rock hit the pane of glass, revealing it as the tapping culprit. I rushed over to the window and looked down. Amanda stood on the ground below my window, a navy blue hoodie tucked down low over her ears. I slid the window open.

"What on earth are you doing down there?" The look on her face was odd, ashen and scared.

"We need to talk. Now. Come down here," she

insisted.

Chapter Forty-Eight

I'll be the first to admit—I was scared to go out there. After my suspicions about Amanda and reading about her father, I really didn't want to go outside with her in the dark. I didn't want to be in the dark *period*, not with a crazy sociopath wreaking havoc in Harrow Hill.

But Amanda was my friend, and I needed to know what was going on. *Was she going to confess?* I wondered wildly. I crept downstairs slowly, afraid of waking my parents. They would be livid if they knew I was sneaking outside at one o'clock in the morning on a school night.

I reached the bottom of the stairs and tiptoed over to the front door. I opened it slowly, cringing as it made a loud creaking noise. I froze, waiting for my mom or dad to come running out of their bedroom to catch me. But that didn't happen.

I slipped out the door, and left it ajar so I could slip back in easily. Amanda was pacing back and forth at the side of the house. "What's going on?" I tried to keep my voice at a whisper.

"I know who did it," she said, looking at me with a serious expression on her face.

"Who?" I asked, flabbergasted.

"How many girls are on the cheerleading team?" She was pacing back and forth rashly. I looked at her blankly. "Just humor me, Dakota."

"Okay. There are six of us." I shrugged. "So what?"

"Tell me the names of everyone the sociopath has targeted," she said.

"Well, me and you." She held up two fingers.

"Monika and Tally," I added, remembering the slashed tires. She held up two more fingers. "And Brittani, with the cat."

She was holding up five fingers total. I still didn't get it.

"Six cheerleaders, five victims…there's only one who hasn't been targeted."

Suddenly, my mind was spinning.

"Genevieve," we both said in unison.

"She egged my grandma's house. Why wouldn't she be doing all of those other things too? And why is she the only cheerleader on the squad who hasn't had any incidents involving the sociopath? She has a lot of reasons to be pissed off. Me…dating Ronnie. You beating out her friends on the squad…" Amanda moved her hands wildly as she talked.

"I can't believe we didn't realize this already. She's the only one…" I said breathlessly.

"Precisely," Amanda said, finally standing still.

We stood there, staring at each other, wondering if our theory was correct.

Chapter Forty-Nine

For the third day in a row, Amanda was standing at the bus stop. "How come you're not riding to school with Ronnie anymore?" I asked. Even though I used to really like Ronnie and I wasn't crazy about them dating, I was still worried about my friend. I also felt terrible for suspecting that it was her doing all of those terrible things just because of her family history. I felt like a jerk, and was going to do my best to be a supportive friend from here on out.

"Ronnie hasn't spoken to me ever since…the fliers," she said, rubbing her hands together nervously. "Screw him. I didn't like him that much anyway." But I could tell she was lying to cover up her feelings.

Amanda shifted her backpack back and forth. "What the heck do you have in that thing? That's the biggest backpack I've ever seen."

"Oh, just stuff I need for class," Amanda

remarked.

We found an empty seat near the back of the bus.

"What do you think we should do about Genevieve? Do you think we should confront her? Tell her we know it's her?" she asked, switching topics. I honestly had no clue what to do about it.

"If we could prove it was her, then we could go to Principal Barlow. But we can't..." I said, my thoughts running away from me. We both sat there quietly, pondering what we should do.

"Thanks for still being my friend," Amanda said out of the blue, catching me completely off guard.

"My dad did some terrible stuff, but that doesn't mean I'm a bad person or a total screw up just because he is. We choose our own fate, and he chose his. I'm going to choose a different path for myself. I'm living with my grandma now and I'm a cheerleader…everything seems to be falling into place…despite Genevieve and some of the kids harassing me. I know I'm rambling, but all I really want to say is thanks for not judging me, Dakota. It really means a lot."

I wasn't sure what to say. "No problem," I nearly whispered.

If she only knew the truth, that I was sitting up late last night reading all about her family on the Internet and judging the hell out of her. Well, I wasn't going to do that anymore.

***

Amanda and I were on the lookout for Genevieve all day, but neither of us had seen her by the time our lunch hour rolled around. Not seeing her during the first part of the school day was not that strange though, because neither of us shared classes with her in the morning. We expected to see her in Phys Ed, but she wasn't there, either.

At cheerleading practice, Coach Davis announced that Genevieve was sick with the flu, and her mother had called in to school this morning.

"Poor baby." Amanda rolled her eyes at me sarcastically. I mouthed the word 'karma' and she grinned.

Coach Davis and Coach Purnell must have reached some sort of agreement, because the boys' basketball team was practicing in the gym again today. We ran through all of our chants and cheers again, but since Genevieve was missing from the formation, it threw everything off.

"Sydney, please come stand in for Genevieve." Coach Davis motioned for her to come join us. She and Ashleigh had learned all of the chants, but they hadn't been involved in learning the half time cheer or stunt.

I hadn't spoken to Sydney since she'd basically admitted to participating in the egging at Amanda's house. I gave her a small smile, despite my reservations. I felt bad that she didn't make the team, and after last night with Amanda, I was starting to think I needed to be less critical of others.

At the end of our routine, we practiced the lift again. Once again, the boys were staring at us. They were mainly staring at me. This time I smiled back at Andy and gave him a little wave. "Dakota, don't wave at boys when you're on top of a stunt," Coach Davis scolded me from below. I could feel my face heat up with embarrassment. I cleared my throat nervously.

One of the boys started whistling at me. When I looked back over at them, I realized it was Ronnie. Andy was giving him a funny look and Amanda looked like she was going to cry.

Chapter Fifty

Friday nights had always been, and always would be, game night in the Densford household. No matter how old I got, I planned on showing up for it. My dad tried to get off work by seven on Fridays just so he could participate. Unfortunately, the weather was too stormy this evening, which meant he was stuck at the station, making sure they didn't go off-air due to wind or water damage on radio transmitters.

Since my brother was still too little to participate, tonight it was just me and Mom. Mom let me pick my favorite game first. I knew it was childish, but my favorite board game was Mouse Trap. The anticipation you felt while turning that crank and waiting to see if your trap worked never got old for me. As usual, I captured Mom's mouse with ease. Even though I was fifteen, I could have sworn she still let me win sometimes.

My mom's favorite game was Clue. While she set up the board, putting all of the little weapons in their respective rooms, I got up for a bathroom break. I also ran upstairs to check my iPhone. Two missed calls from an unknown number. But there were no voicemails or texts to go with the calls, which was unusual for any of my friends.

I went back downstairs and kicked Mom's butt at Clue. "I think I'm going to turn in early, sweetheart. I have to work for a few hours this weekend to get caught up with some of my paperwork. I'm taking off for your games on Tuesday and Friday, so I need to get as much done as I can over the weekend." She yawned.

"You're the best, Mom." I kissed her on the cheek before heading up to my own bed. It was after ten o'clock, but I didn't feel tired. I tried playing a few apps on my phone, but nothing held my interest. I was all gamed out for the night.

I stuck my ear buds in, flipping through my phone, looking for a song that I wasn't totally sick of. I picked a song by Miley Cyrus, one of those catchy beats that never gets old. If I hadn't been looking at my phone at that exact moment, I would have missed the call coming in with the ear buds in. It was that number again.

I hit the 'Accept' button. "Hello?"

The voice on the other end was strange and robotic. It had to be some sort of recording or someone talking through an electronic voice recorder.

"If you go to the game, you will die," the creepy voice warned.

"I know it's you, Genevieve!" When I said her name, she hung up on the other end. Ten minutes later my phone rang again. But this time it was

Amanda.

As soon as I answered, she asked, "Have you gotten any weird phone calls?"

"Yes. Don't worry. It's just Genevieve. We need to ignore her. If we get scared, she wins, because that's exactly what she's trying to do."

"But why wouldn't she want us to come to the game on Tuesday? We're on the same squad!"

"Because she hates us," I reminded her.

"Oh yeah."

We hung up a few moments later. Even though I was a little scared, I was so tired that I fell asleep with my ear buds in. I slept like a baby.

Chapter Fifty-One

On Saturday, I received another strange call. Only this one wasn't from Genevieve. It was Ronnie. I hadn't heard his voice in so long that I didn't know who it was at first.

"I was wondering if you'd like to meet at that sushi place by your house. I know you love sushi," he said, his voice shaky.

"I thought you had a girlfriend. Or *girlfriends*, I should say. One week you're with Genevieve and then I saw you with Amanda."

"It's always been you, Dakota. I saw you standing on the top of that pyramid the other day, and I knew I had to have you back. Meet me for lunch. Please?"

How could I say no to that?

"Okay. You want to meet at our usual booth, the one in the back corner?"

"Sure. See you soon, babe," he said, hanging up. The sushi restaurant was only a block away. Now I had to decide what to wear for this exciting occasion!

***

When I stepped out the front door, I was thrilled to see the sun was shining. I'd taken the time to curl my hair into little ringlets, and I didn't want it ruined by rain. Even though I'd fixed my hair, I was dressed casually in jeans, flip-flops, and a mint green blouse. It took me less than five minutes to get to the restaurant where I was meeting Ronnie.

I could see his Trans Am parked in the front parking lot—parked in a handicapped slot, no less. As soon as I entered, I saw him in the back booth, just as we'd planned. He looked handsome in a dark green polo and jeans. I slipped in the booth across from him.

"I ordered for you," he said, pleased with himself.

"Thanks," I said quietly.

"I'm glad you decided to come. I knew you didn't really like that guy, Andy. He's such a freaking dork." Ronnie chuckled, holding up his hand for the waitress.

"Yeah, he is," I agreed. A pretty, petite Asian waitress brought a pitcher of water and club crackers to the table. For some reason, they always brought crackers and water to the table first. I was grateful for the water today.

"Hey, asshole!" Amanda suddenly shouted, stomping toward our table heatedly.

"How did she know I was here?" Ronnie looked

at me, confused.

"Because I called her." I smiled up at my best friend. Amanda smiled back.

Then she picked up the pitcher of water and emptied its contents over his head.

We locked arms, walking out of there with our heads held high.

"That couldn't have gone any better," I said, rolling with laughter.

"What a douche." Amanda shook her head back and forth.

"We got him good. He finally got put in his place. I've been waiting for a chance to do that for longer than you even know!" I told her, smiling as I imagined the water pouring over his head and the look on his face as he sat there, stunned.

"Thanks for calling to tell me. I'm so glad I did that! I feel so much better too! You want to come over?" Amanda asked.

"Maybe later. My mom's taking me over to Andy's to finish our history project. It's due on Monday."

"Do you like Andy a lot?" She raised her eyebrows at me.

"I'm crazy about him," I realized.

Andy might be a dork, but he was *my* dork.

Chapter Fifty-Two

Last Monday was exciting because of tryouts, but this Monday ran a close second because my uniform was coming in today! It was my second uniform of the season, but hopefully, my last. I knocked lightly on Coach Davis's door. The bell for first period hadn't rung yet, and Coach Davis was sitting at her desk with her head in her hands, deep in thought. Even though she was a tough coach, Coach Davis had grown on me. I couldn't wait to have her as an English teacher next year.

"Come in, Dakota." She waved me into the room.

"I'm sorry to bother you, Coach. I just wanted to check and see if my uniform had arrived yet," I said, my voice pleading. I was dying to try it on for the first time!

"The uniforms will be here by ten o'clock. Amanda, Monika, and Genevieve's altered uniforms will be here at ten, also. Because of what happened to your uniform before, I would prefer to keep all of the uniforms in my classroom until the end of the day. I will pass them out at practice."

She made a good point. I didn't want anything to happen to this uniform either. If keeping it safe meant waiting until the end of the day, so be it.

"Now that I have you here, Dakota, we need to discuss something important." Her voice sounded serious all of a sudden. "Genevieve will be unable to attend tomorrow's game. She's been admitted to the hospital."

"Oh, no!" I suddenly felt bad for all the terrible things I said about her. "What happened to her?" A nervous feeling was forming in my gut.

"Remember how she was displaying flu-like symptoms? Well, her symptoms got worse yesterday. Her mother called me last night and said that the doctors suspect she may have been poisoned."

I gasped.

"Poisoned?" I shook my head in disbelief.

Amanda and I were wrong. The sociopath had victimized all six of us, including Genevieve. At least now I knew that Genevieve wasn't our culprit.

Chapter Fifty-Three

All I wanted to do right then was track down Amanda and tell her the awful news, but I had to go to my Biology class first. I took my seat, pulling out my heavy textbook. I could hear Miss Grimes explaining the difference between DNA and RNA, but I wasn't listening to a word of the lesson.

How could we have been so wrong? And why would someone try to poison Genevieve? Were they trying to kill her when they did it? This was all getting way too serious and out of hand. A prank is one thing, but attempted murder?

I thought about the voice on the phone, warning me not to go to the game. If the caller wasn't Genevieve, then who was it? A chill ran up my spine as I remembered the weirdo breathing heavily through my stall door.

As soon as the bell rang, I went in search of Amanda. I had to tell her what was going on. As I waded through the hallway full of people, I saw

Amanda and Monika talking by Amanda's locker. When she turned around to face me, I knew she'd already heard the news. Her face looked ashen.

"Dakota!" I hurried over to her side.

"Coach Davis pulled all of us out of class to tell us about Genevieve. She said that she told you first." I nodded glumly. Tally came walking down the hall. She must have heard the news too, because she came over to join us.

"This is all so crazy and terrible," Monika said, shaking her head in disbelief.

"I know! Now our cheers are going to be screwed up. Sydney had better be able to learn the cheers," Tally said, flipping her light blonde hair over her shoulder snobbishly. We all looked at her, shocked.

"I meant it's terrible what happened to Genevieve, not that our cheers will be altered," Monika scolded Tally.

"She has a point though. This is Sydney's lucky day. She might get a spot on the team after all," Amanda muttered.

I looked at Amanda incredulously. Her remark was insensitive, but it rang with truth. Sydney did stand to gain the most from Genevieve's illness. Could my former best friend be the one responsible for all of this? I wasn't certain, but I had to find out for myself.

Chapter Fifty-Four

"Did you do it?" I asked Sydney bluntly, stopping her crudely in the hallway. I'd known she had Geometry for third period, so I waited for her at the doorway to her class. She narrowed her eyes at me.

"Did I do *what*, Dakota?" She placed her hands on her hips defensively.

"Did you try to kill Genevieve?" I asked boldly. Sydney's eyes grew round as quarters.

"Dakota, you are crazy! You have really lost your mind! All you've done since school started is blame me for one thing after another! I'm starting to think it's *you* doing all of this crazy stuff!" She poked a finger at my chest angrily.

People were staring at us now, and they were looking at me like I was a lunatic. This was not going as planned. I turned around and walked away. What else could I do? It's not like I had proof of anything.

Maybe I am acting like a lunatic, I considered, feeling slightly embarrassed.

My next class was American History and I was going to be late. I had to pick up the pace because mine and Andy's Joan of Arc project was due today! I skidded through the doorway, plopping in my seat just as the final bell rang. I let out a sigh of relief. Andy looked at me and raised his eyebrows questioningly. "Tell you later," I said, exasperated.

Our project was not the only one due today, and we had to sit and listen to three other groups go before us. I couldn't even tell you who the historical figures were being presented—my brain was somewhere else. When I heard our names being called, I was completely spaced out. I jumped up in surprise.

I helped Andy carry our tri-fold board up to the front of the room. We were supposed to take turns presenting the material, and I'd written down my parts on note cards.

My note cards! I realized in horror that I'd been so distracted chasing Sydney down between periods, that I'd left the cards in my locker. Panic rose in my chest.

Andy immediately sensed something was wrong. "I forgot my note cards," I confessed under my breath as we stood in front of the class setting up the board.

"Take mine. I'll do your parts," he said, shoving his cards in my hand before I had a chance to refuse.

Chapter Fifty-Five

If kissing were allowed at school, I'd have grabbed Andy and given him a smooch right then and there. "You saved my butt in there," I said gratefully, slamming my locker door closed.

"That's what boyfriends are for." He slipped his hand in mine, steering me toward the lunch room.

I was so happy walking with Andy that I'd nearly forgotten about Genevieve's poisoning. I filled Andy in on what Coach Davis had told me this morning. "That's terrifying," he admitted, shaking his head in wonderment. "Was she poisoned while eating lunch at school?"

I stopped dead in my tracks. That was something I hadn't thought of.

"I honestly have no idea. I don't know if anyone knows when it happened, or why. But I think I know the 'why' part. Someone is jealous of the girls who made the squad. It's one thing to play little pranks, but what they did to Genevieve is just downright crazy."

I had to agree with him.

"Don't worry. I brought my lunch from home, and it's completely safe. It came from my own personal fridge, so nobody's touched it," he offered, pulling out bologna sandwiches and chips.

But I wasn't listening. I was thinking about the phone calls Amanda and I received over the weekend.

I told Andy about the menacing voice on the phone, and how they said I would die if I went to the game on Tuesday. It was his turn to stop dead in his tracks.

"Have you told anyone about this?" His eyes grew wide with concern. I shook my head, suddenly feeling foolish.

"I probably should have told someone right away. I just didn't realize at the time how serious things had gotten."

"Come on. We need to talk to Principal Barlow." He squeezed my hand, leading me to her office.

Chapter Fifty-Six

The first thing Principal Barlow did was contact the Harrow Hill police department. A heavyset, white-haired detective spoke to me and Amanda in Principal Barlow's office. His name was Detective Simms, and he was slightly intimidating with a gruff voice and stiff gait.

Detective Simms also called in the other girls from the squad, to see if any of them had received similar calls. No one else had, besides me and Amanda. "We're investigating all of these crimes."

Hearing him call the sociopath's pranks 'crimes' really put everything in perspective. This was serious.

I showed Detective Simms my cell phone, as did Amanda. Whoever had made the threatening phone calls was smart enough to block their numbers. "If we cancel the ball game because of these threats, then we're doing exactly what the perpetrator wants us to do," Detective Simms said.

"But does that really matter? This isn't a contest! We're talking about the safety of our children!" Principal Barlow exclaimed, looking down at Brittani, her eyes filled with worry. Detective Simms stuck out a hand to stop her.

"I understand that, ma'am. But if we cancel the game, then it will simply encourage the perpetrator. He or she will do it again when the next game comes around. And the next game. And the next. And so on." Principal Barlow looked defeated.

"I'll bring several deputies with me to the game tomorrow night. We'll keep an eye on all of you girls, and everyone that attends."

He turned to us. "We will keep you all safe. But in the meantime, I want all of you to be cautious and aware of your surroundings at all times. Report anything strange or any other incidences to me directly." We nodded, all of us wearing masks of confusion.

Walking out of Principal Barlow's office, I should have felt better. Safer. Instead, I was becoming more and more convinced that we were all in grave danger.

Chapter Fifty-Seven

By the time I went to practice at the end of the day, I'd nearly forgotten about my new uniform. It was lying draped over the bleachers when I walked into the gym. There was also a new bodysuit underneath it and a brand new set of sparkly pompoms beside it. I thought my first uniform looked great, but this one was ten times better. The color of the fabric was bright and bold; it was obviously brand spanking new. *I have the nicest uniform on the squad*, I realized, suddenly feeling excited for the opening game tomorrow, despite Detective Simms' concerns.

The other girls' altered uniforms were also waiting for them. I saw one with Monika's name on it and another one for Tally. Then I saw Genevieve's freshly altered uniform lying on a section of the bench by itself. My stomach filled with dread, and I was overcome with feelings of remorse for saying so many bad things about her when, as it turns out, she was a victim of this crazy person too.

"Sydney, you'll be wearing Genevieve's uniform tomorrow at the game. She's taller than you, so it may be a little long on you," Coach Davis explained. I jerked around to look at my former best friend.

"It will be fine," Sydney replied, pushing past me and walking over to the bench to retrieve her uniform. She held it against her front side, smiling. When she saw me still looking at her, she narrowed her eyes and set it back down on the bench.

I still couldn't shake my suspicions of Sydney. "It was her. I'm sure of it," Amanda whispered to me.

"I don't know. We jumped the gun when we suspected Genevieve. We need to be careful not to do that again," I warned. I was also warning myself when I said it.

Coach Davis had us stretch first, and then we practiced our back tucks for the halftime routine. We went through all of the cheers again, mainly for Sydney's benefit. She caught on quickly and had no trouble learning the cheers. That didn't surprise me. Sydney was a good cheerleader, even if she didn't make the main squad.

Maybe she's mad because she feels like she got the shaft, and that's why she poisoned Genevieve, a little voice nagged. It still seemed a little extreme, even for Sydney.

We reviewed the halftime cheer. Sydney replaced Genevieve in the back of the lift. It was her job to make sure that I didn't fall backwards, which was a pretty important job, if you asked me. I was worried that she might drop me on purpose like Brittani did to Teresa, but she performed her role as a spotter perfectly.

I looked at her, my old best friend, as we gathered up our items to go home. I just couldn't believe she'd do something like that, I really couldn't. "See you at the game tomorrow, girls!" Coach Davis shouted, letting us know that practice was over.

I followed Sydney out of the gym. She turned left down the west wing hallway, and I knew she must be heading to her locker. I followed closely behind. Finally reaching her locker, she turned the dial to enter the combination.

"What do you want, Dakota?" she growled, without even looking back over her shoulder.

"I'm sorry, Syd. We were such good friends. *Best* friends. Maybe I *have* been a little paranoid lately," I admitted.

"*Maybe*?" she said, giving me a crooked smile.

She swung her locker door open. When she did, dozens of white fliers fell out to the floor.

They were the fliers with the pictures of Amanda and her dad on them. I looked up at Sydney, stunned. I took off running down the hallway, trying to put as much distance between me and her as possible.

Chapter Fifty-Eight

I told Amanda and my mom about the fliers in Sydney's locker. I also told my mom about Genevieve being poisoned. The look of terror on her face made me uneasy. If my mom was this worried, then I knew it was bad because she usually stayed pretty calm in most situations. I felt bad for causing her to worry so much.

"Honey, I know you're trying to help, but just because Sydney had some of those fliers in her locker, it doesn't necessarily mean that she was responsible for what happened to Genevieve, or the cat incident. You know what I've always told you about jumping to conclusions. It sounds like you need to let Detective Simms do his job and try not to figure out who's doing this." She gave me a stern look in the rearview mirror.

"But Mom…"

"No, Dakota. I'm serious. You don't need to get involved any more than you already have to be. I don't want you drawing any more attention to yourself than you have to...I don't want the sociopath to fixate on you."

We rode home in silence, her terrifying words hanging in the air like a black cloud. I could tell that my mom was a nervous wreck. Amanda looked anxious too, chewing on her lower lip, deep in thought. She'd barely spoken since I'd shared the story about the fliers with her.

"Do you need help carrying your gear inside?" I asked as we pulled up in front of her house to drop her off. She shook her head. She was weighed down with her cheerleading gear and that monstrous-sized backpack.

"I'll call you later," she said, a blank look on her face.

"I can't wait to see you try on your new uniform," my mom said as we pulled into the garage. I knew she was just trying to cheer me up. Honestly though, despite everything, I couldn't wait to try it on either.

My mom waited downstairs while I went up to my room to change. I pulled on the body suit and a pair of bloomers, and then I slipped the top on over my head. I pulled the skirt up over my hips.

The uniform fit snugly and was pretty skimpy, but it looked fantastic. My curvy figure filled it out perfectly. I picked up the pompoms and stood in front of the full length mirror. I took a deep breath. I was hit with a feeling of unexpected joy. All I could do now was hope that the sociopath didn't try to screw up my happiness on game night tomorrow.

Chapter Fifty-Nine

The morning sun shone down through my open curtains and I could feel its heat on my skin. For a day that was supposed to be filled with impending doom, it sure was beautiful outside. The skies were cloud-free and it was unseasonably warm. I wore a Harrow Dragons tank top over black capris to show my school support for game day. I glanced at the uniform hanging up in my closet and the pompoms lying on my computer chair. *I'll be damned if I'm going to let some crazy person ruin my first game as a Harrow varsity cheerleader,* I decided firmly.

When I went downstairs for breakfast, my mom was packing my lunch. "I don't want you eating at school until this person is caught." She was slicing a ham and provolone sandwich in half, just the way I liked it. I'll never understand why sandwiches always taste better when moms make them.

I thought about Amanda and her mom, who was God knows where, and her crazy Grandma Mimi.

"Mom, would you mind packing a lunch for Amanda too?"

"Sure." She pulled out more lunchmeat and cheese.

My mom made a good point. If Genevieve was poisoned at school, it probably was best to avoid cafeteria food for a while. Amanda and I rode to school with our lunch sacks in silence, both of us feeling an odd mixture of excitement and fear for the day ahead.

"Did you try on your uniform last night?" She nodded, and her lips formed a tiny smile.

"It looked great. Fit perfectly," she admitted.

"Mine did too. Let's just try to enjoy today."

She nodded, taking her arm in mine as we walked through the entrance of the school.

Andy was waiting for me.

"I want to stick by your side today," he said, his face etched with concern.

"I guess I'll allow that," I joked, unable to hold back a grin.

"He's a keeper," Amanda said, and she was right. I felt lucky to have such an amazing boyfriend and best friend.

Speaking of best friends, Sydney passed by, walking alone as I headed to Biology. She tried to catch my eye, but I ignored her. If she was the sociopath, I didn't want to be anywhere near her. I was going to take my mom's advice and just try not to get involved. Hopefully, Detective Simms would eventually be able to catch the person who did this, and then we wouldn't have to worry anymore.

Chapter Sixty

Throughout the day, I recognized several police officers patrolling the hallways. Seeing them brought the butterflies back to my stomach, but I was grateful for their diligence. Perhaps making their presence known was what prevented the sociopath from striking again because the day went by with zero incidents.

I'd grown so accustomed to having practice after school that I nearly headed down to the gym when the final bell rang. But then I remembered that it was game night, and I had to go home and get ready for it.

Amanda and I got ready together at my house. We had to be there by six o'clock—tip off was at six-thirty.

"How does my hair look?" She looked up from the mirror to face me.

"Beautiful," I answered honestly, admiring her short, trendy hairdo. She had gold barrettes pinned on the sides to hold back her bangs, and the back of her hair was sprayed into a stylish poof. My hair was pulled into a tight, high ponytail with curls and a gold bow.

"You look great too." She smiled back at me.

We painted our faces with makeup and glitter, smoothing lotion over our legs before slipping our uniforms on.

"Let's take a selfie!" Amanda stood up, positioning her phone in front of our faces.

"Say 'Go Dragons'!" I cried.

"Go Dragons!" we squealed in unison.

I looked at my Hello Kitty alarm clock. It was quarter 'til six. "Time to get going!" we cried happily. Gathering up our pompoms and bags, we headed out to my mom's car.

Today's the day!

Chapter Sixty-One

When we entered the gym, I immediately knew something was different. This place, where we'd been practicing for weeks now, looked and sounded like a whole new world. The boys were on the floor, but they looked serious now in their red and gold uniforms. The sounds of that round ball pounding the wooden court and the sweet swishing sound of the net made it unmistakable—it was game night!

The boys were warming up and the bleachers were still mostly empty, but I could feel the tension and excitement in the air. I saw Andy practicing layups. He looked gorgeous in his uniform and Jordan high tops. I waved at him. When I caught his eye, I shouted, "Good luck!"

Monika and Tally were stretching on the sidelines. Amanda and I joined them. "Are you guys excited?" Monika asked sweetly.

We both nodded. I'd nearly forgotten that this wasn't Monika and Tally's first year at this. They were pros—this was their fourth year cheering for the Harrow Dragons.

"Have you guys seen Coach Davis?" I looked around the gym.

"She's right over there." Tally pointed to an area by the concession stands. Coach Davis and Coach Purnell were talking to Detective Simms and two other officers I hadn't seen before.

"Is everything okay?" Amanda asked.

"I think so. I think they're just discussing safety procedures," Monika reassured us.

"Does anyone know how Genevieve is doing?" Amanda asked.

"I spoke to her mom last night. She's still in the hospital, but she's doing much better. She was dehydrated after vomiting so much, and they had to give her an IV for fluids."

I cringed at the thought of Genevieve lying in a hospital bed with a needle in her arm on game night instead of being here with us where she belonged. Genevieve and I might have had our differences over the years, but she was a member of our team and I didn't want any physical harm to come to her. Based on the worried look on Amanda's face, she felt the same way.

"Hey, team!" Brittani squealed feverishly, running across the floor to join us. *I guess I have to be nice to Brittani since she's my teammate too*, I thought with a sigh.

Even though I wanted to simply forget about what she did to Teresa, I just couldn't. Actually, I could see *her* being the sociopath, if she had not been a victim herself. Brittani got down on the floor and started stretching with us. She smiled at me and I tried to smile back.

People were pouring into the gym now and taking their seats in the stands. I recognized several of my classmates and some of their parents. I waved to Mr. Thompson, my Spanish teacher. "*Buena suerte!*" he called out to me from his spot in the stands. I had no idea what that meant.

"It means good luck," Brittani whispered behind me.

"Gracias!" I waved back to him.

"Thanks, Brit," I said, flashing a grateful smile at her.

The scoreboard lit up and the opposing team, the Crimson Cougars, came out onto the floor to warm up. Their cheerleaders also came out of the locker room area and took their place on the sidelines opposite us. They eyeballed us, and we did the same. My mom came in with my baby brother in tow, and found a spot close behind me. I looked at the clock. The game would begin in five minutes. *Where the heck is Sydney?* I wondered.

Chapter Sixty-Two

Coach Davis took a seat on the bleachers. "Get ready to start the cheers, just as we practiced, girls!"

I noticed Detective Simms standing near the exit doors. On the other side of the gym were two more officers, scouring the crowd for anything suspicious. The game was starting in one minute.

"Where's Sydney?" I asked Coach Davis. Her eyes widened as she realized what I already had—there were only five of us. Suddenly, Ashleigh came running into the gym at a full sprint. Her quick pace put the officers on guard and they were looking our way.

"Sorry, guys!" she said, getting in line beside us. She was out of breath from running. "Sorry I'm late." She was dressed in Genevieve's uniform—the same uniform Sydney was supposed to be wearing tonight.

"What are you doing here, Ashleigh?" Coach Davis demanded.

"You don't know?" Ashleigh looked from Coach Davis to us with a confused expression.

"Know what?" Coach Davis made a 'hurry up' motion with her hands as she looked up at the clock.

"Sydney called me an hour ago, asked me to pick up the uniform from her house," Ashleigh explained.

"Oh my god. Please tell me she hasn't been poisoned too!" Amanda's eyes widened.

"No. All she said was that she couldn't cheer tonight. She said she had to deal with a family situation. Her exact words were 'I'm stuck and I can't go to the game.'" Ashleigh shrugged.

"Okay, girls. We'll discuss this later. It's time to cheer!" Coach Davis announced just as the buzzer rang.

Chapter Sixty-Three

I cheered my heart out during the game, loving every minute of it. For a while, I almost forgot about the sociopath. Our boys were playing beautifully, leading at half time by nearly fifteen points. We kept the crowd excited, chanting cheers as loudly, and with as much pep, as we could muster.

Ashleigh did a great job filling in for Genevieve. I was a little worried about her doing the lift at the halftime show, considering the fact that she'd never fully practiced it, but the routine went perfectly. We nailed all of our back tucks and the stunt was fantastic. At the end of the routine, our audience roared with cheers and applause. It was the greatest feeling in the world.

I loved the way my mom smiled as she watched me. I could see the pride just pouring out of her in waves. I'd hoped to see my dad tonight, but I knew that if it were possible, then he would have come.

The final score was 51 to 42, Dragons. I was excited for Andy as he raced across the floor at the sound of the last buzzer. We'd won our first game of the season!

The opposing players smacked palms respectively, and then Andy ran toward me, gathering me up in a big bear hug. Coach Davis had said no flirting during stunts, but she didn't say no flirting on the court.

I leaned in and placed my lips on his. He was surprised, but happy, and kissed me back lovingly. The sociopath had tried his best to ruin this night, but nothing could take away from what Andy and I shared.

Chapter Sixty-Four

After the game, my mom dropped me, Andy, and Amanda at Pete's Pizza Palace. She said she was going home to change and feed my little brother, and then would be back to pick us up. What she was really doing was giving me some space with my friends, and I appreciated her effort.

I'm going to miss her driving me around when I get my license next year, I realized for the second time in weeks.

We were still revved up from the game as we took a seat in a booth near the back of the pizza parlor. Dozens of our other classmates were pouring in through the doors of the restaurant. *I guess this is the after game hangout*, I realized. I saw Monika and Tally with their boyfriends sitting at a corner table. I waved.

Andy, Amanda, and I couldn't reach an agreement on what type of pizza we wanted, so we asked if they could do it one-third cheese, one-third pepperoni, and one-third sausage. The waitress laughed and rolled her eyes, but obliged.

Amanda wandered off toward a group of arcade games. I suspected that she too was trying to give me and my boyfriend some space. Andy and I discussed some of the game's highlights and the basketball team's upcoming opponent, the Brownstown Bears. I was enjoying the conversation, but my mind kept drifting back to Sydney's absence from the game.

What sort of family problems would prevent her from showing up? I wondered. I remembered the look on her face when she was fingering that uniform at practice yesterday. She'd been so excited to fill in for Genevieve. *Why would she not show up?*

"I just can't help wondering what happened to Sydney tonight," I said aloud, scratching my head.

"Yeah, I was wondering that too. Why did she leave before the game started?" Andy asked, taking a bite of the cheesy pizza.

"That's the thing! She never even showed up. She told Ashleigh she was stuck doing something—something to do with a family situation."

"Whoa! That's strange because I got to the gym early to practice my three-point shot, and Sydney was there too. She said she wanted to practice all the cheers for tonight, to make sure they were perfect."

My mouth fell open. "What's going on?" I threw my hands up in frustration. "Was she wearing her uniform?"

He nodded. This whole story was becoming

more and more bizarre.

I dug my iPhone out of my cheer bag and dialed Sydney's cell phone number. It went straight to voicemail. Since that didn't work, I called her mom and dad's home number. Her mother, Lacey, answered on the first ring.

"Sydney, is that you?" she blurted into the phone, without even saying hello.

"No, Mrs. Hargreaves. It's Dakota Densford. Did you drop Sydney off at the game tonight?" I tried not to sound too alarmed.

"Yes, I did. She was supposed to get a hold of me when she was ready for me to pick her up, but she still hasn't called. Have you seen her?"

"Not yet," I said, hanging up.

I turned to look at Andy and Amanda, who had just wandered back to the table and were looking at me strangely. "We have to go back to school. Something's wrong. I think Sydney is in trouble."

Chapter Sixty-Five

Harrow High was two blocks from Pete's Pizza Palace. I ran.

Amanda and Andy did their best to keep up with me. Something was very wrong. My spidey senses were kicking in.

When we got to the school, it was deserted. However, the front doors were still unlocked due to tonight's game and the nighttime cleaning staff. I ran through the empty hallways, headed for the gym. Andy and Amanda followed right behind me. They didn't ask any questions because they simply trusted my judgment. That's why I loved them so much.

"Search the boys' locker room," I commanded Andy. Amanda and I headed into the girls' locker room. We opened every locker and looked under every bench. No Sydney.

"Her locker is at the other end of school. Let's go down there and look. Maybe she got hurt down there by her locker and she's in some sort of trouble," I said, thinking out loud.

"Let's go," Amanda said. Andy was waiting outside of the door for us.

"Did you find anything?"

"Nothing besides stinky gym socks and used jock straps." I gave him a look. This wasn't the time for his sense of humor.

"Sorry." He gave me a sheepish look.

We headed down the west wing hallway toward Sydney's locker. It was dark and eerily deserted. As we got closer to our destination, I could have sworn that I heard a muffled cry.

I froze. "Did you hear that sound?" I asked Andy and Amanda.

"Yeah. But whatever it is, it's coming from the other hallway." Amanda pointed down a narrow hall that led in a different direction from Sydney's locker.

"Okay. Let's go that way then."

A few steps later, I heard the sound again. Running toward it, I recognized the hallway. Suddenly, I knew where the sound was coming from—Ashleigh's locker.

Chapter Sixty-Six

There was a person inside the locker and regrettably, I knew who it was. I started banging on the locker, trying to open it. The muffled cries grew louder and louder. Whoever was in there could hear us.

"Oh my god! How are we going to get it open? We'll get you out of there, Ashleigh, don't worry!" Amanda screamed. Andy started kicking at the locker furiously, pushing me aside.

"We could stand here guessing combinations all night long and still never get the right one," he said, frustrated.

I suddenly remembered something. For once, Brittani Barlow had done something positive. She'd told me about the binder in her mother's office, the one with everyone's locker combinations written down inside of it.

"Stay here." I took off running down the hall. "And call Detective Simms while I'm gone!" I added over my shoulder. I reached Principal Barlow's door within minutes. It was dark, deserted. I started beating and kicking at the door furiously.

Like most teachers' doors, it had a narrow pane of glass on the upper section of the door. I knew what I had to do if I wanted to get that binder. I grabbed a student chair from the hall. It had metal tips on its feet. I lifted up the chair and slammed the feet against the pane as hard as I could. A small portion of the glass shattered. I used the tips of the chair to knock away loose glass shards, and then I stuck my arm through the opening, unlocking the door.

I felt around in the dark until I found a light switch. I turned it on, immediately spotting several large binders on Principal Barlow's desk. I opened up each one wildly, throwing aside the ones that were not it. Finally, I opened a pale yellow binder and saw the combinations typed in rows. Bingo!

I knew Ashleigh's combo would be on the bottom of the list under W's for her last name: Westerfield. *Jackpot!*

I ripped the whole sheet out and raced back down the hall. Amanda and Andy were still standing by the locker. "The police are on their way," Andy told me. *Thank God.*

Amanda was still standing, her mouth pressed against the locker door, trying to give words of encouragement. "Step aside," I ordered. "And by the way, it's not Ashleigh in there."

"Huh?" Amanda stared at me, baffled.

I started turning the dial, looking down at the numbers displayed on the paper from Principal

Barlow's office. I was trying to stay calm, but my fingers were shaking uncontrollably. And that's when I heard a new sound…heavy boots moving down an adjacent hallway. They moved slowly, confidently. Someone was coming for us!

Chapter Sixty-Seven

"Don't move!" I heard someone scream from down the hallway.

"Now, *that* is Ashleigh." I turned toward the voice, fuming. I was going to kick her ass for shoving one of my best friends into a locker.

Ashleigh was standing there in the darkness, holding something in her hand. A glimmer of something silvery caused me to freeze in place. Was she going to *shoot* me if I opened the locker? Surely, she didn't have a gun?

As she took a step forward, moving into the light, I finally saw what was really in her hand. A metal object, but not a gun. It looked like…*a crowbar?*

The last thing I wanted was to get hit by a crowbar, but it wasn't like she was holding a gun, so I turned back to the locker and started quickly turning the dial again.

"Don't!" Ashleigh screamed, running toward me

like a maniac. I heard the sound of the lock unlatching, and as I threw open the locker door, I saw Ashleigh a few feet away from me. She had the crowbar ready to swing, raised high over her head.

"Ashleigh, *don't*!" I heard Andy and Amanda screaming.

"Go, run!" Andy nudged me.

But I didn't run. I did something Ashleigh wasn't expecting. I charged straight at her. This was the person who'd been making my life a living hell, and that all ended tonight. No way was I running from this maniac!

I reached for the crowbar, grasping for it desperately with both hands. My hands met cold metal, and I jerked hard, trying to wrestle the crowbar from her hand. We fell to the floor, rolling around wildly, both of us refusing to release the weapon. Amanda screamed shrilly, and then Andy was behind Ashleigh, pulling the crowbar away.

"Ashleigh Westerfield, put your hands in the air!" Detective Simms hollered, racing down the hall to my rescue. I let go of the crowbar, and so did Andy. But Ashleigh ignored the detective's pleas, and swung the metal at my face.

That's when Detective Simms shot her.

Chapter Sixty-Eight

By the time we got the locker open, Sydney's face was blue from oxygen deprivation. Now I understood why Ashleigh had said that Sydney was "stuck" and couldn't attend the game. She was stuffed inside the locker so tightly that we had to wait for paramedics to come wedge her out.

Sydney had been hit over the head with Ashleigh's metal crowbar, and her wound required nearly two dozen stitches. The most damage done was to her mental state. She was in complete shock when they pulled her out, with her eyes wide open from being frozen with fear. At first, I thought she was dead.

After Ashleigh knocked Sydney out with the crowbar, she apparently stripped off her uniform and stuffed her in the locker half-naked. She was wearing only her bra and underwear when we found her. I couldn't even imagine the terror she must have felt, waking up in that tight, dark locker. I don't even want to think about it.

Sydney was in the hospital for several days. When I went to see her she was very appreciative for the role I played in saving her. She actually called me her hero. I was just appreciative of the fact that she actually forgave me for being such a jerk of a friend.

As it turned out, the reason she had all of those fliers in her locker was because she'd been going around, taking them down that day, just like Amanda and I had been. She said that she wanted to help take the fliers down because she felt guilty for sitting in the car on the night that Genevieve, Tasha, and Mariella egged Amanda's house. She admitted that Tasha wrote the note to Amanda's Grandma Mimi and signed my name. "I think we are all even now, don't you?" I joked, holding my best friend's hand tightly in mine.

I also sustained an injury that night, but it was fairly minor. Without even realizing it, or feeling the pain, I'd sliced my arm on the jagged edges of the glass in Principal Barlow's door. I had to get several stitches and wear it wrapped in gauze for a week, which made cheerleading slightly difficult. But all in all, I felt very fortunate that was the only harm that came to me.

Ashleigh was arrested right there in the hallway of Harrow High. Lucky for her, Detective Simms had terrific aim, and he aimed for her big toe when he shot her. He stopped her from hitting me with the crowbar, but he avoided a deadly shot.

When they placed the cuffs around her wrists, Ashleigh was still wearing Genevieve's cheerleading uniform. Strangely, she yelled, "Go, Dragons!", as she was hauled out to the patrol car. She was charged with two counts of attempted murder, along with a laundry list of minor charges.

She confessed to tearing up my uniform and admitted to memorizing my combination that day when we were standing at my locker, and she was giving me that speech about how happy she was even though she didn't make the squad. Go figure. Looking back at it now, I felt like I should have known. I'd never seen someone act so happy to *not* make the cheerleading team, and it all made sense to me now.

Ashleigh also fessed up to stuffing a cat that she murdered herself in Brittani's gym bag while Brittani was outside playing tennis during Phys Ed. Ashleigh further admitted to slipping Ricin powder into Genevieve's power drink at lunch, and slicing the tires of Monika and Tally's vehicles. Apparently, you could buy anything on the Internet, including poison.

As it turns out, my mom's psychological profile was sort of right. Ashleigh's father had been physically abusing her for years, and that's why she always wore big, baggy clothes to cover up her body at school. Her mother was a severe alcoholic. Ashleigh was very manipulative and she had us all fooled. And she certainly showed no remorse for her wrongdoings, just like my mom said would be the case. When they asked her why she did it, she simply smiled and said, "I did it for the team." I still get the creeps just thinking about it.

Regardless of Ashleigh's background, I wished

she would have chosen a different fate. She was actually a decent cheerleader, and with Monika and Tally graduating this year, she would have certainly made the squad next year. I guess she just couldn't handle being an alternate anymore. She wanted to be on the team so badly she was willing to kill for it. Literally!

Deep down, I couldn't help feeling a little sorry for her. Maybe I was destined to join the social work field just like my mother, after all. Either that, or I might be a cop. Detective Simms' bravery that night was inspiring, to say the least.

Ashleigh was dealt a bad hand in life with her parents. However, every time I looked at my best friend, Amanda, I couldn't help but think about her familial background too. Amanda, unlike Ashleigh, had defied the odds, and would never be a bad egg, like her parents. I felt awful for suspecting her, and I planned on *never* telling her that fact.

Ashleigh did teach me one thing when it came to my favorite sport—it's just cheerleading! It's not life or death, and not worth losing friends over. It certainly wasn't worth risking our lives for. I decided to never take my friends or family for granted ever again, because as I learned recently with Sydney, they could be taken away from me in the blink of an eye over any little crazy reason.

Chapter Sixty-Nine

Two Weeks Later…

It was ten minutes 'til game time, and Harrow's varsity cheerleading squad was having a powwow. Two weeks had passed since Sydney's near-death experience, and even though we were all still a little shaken, we couldn't help feeling pumped up for game night. After all, this is what we'd been waiting for!

We were waiting for Brittani and Coach Davis to show up. Coach Davis was busy chatting it up with Coach Purnell. A few days ago, she showed up at practice with a big rock on her finger, and we all know who the lucky guy must be—Coach Purnell, of course!

I was smiling at the two coaches dreamily when Andy walked past me with a basketball tucked under his arm. "They started out as high school sweethearts, you know…" he said in passing, a big cheesy grin on his face.

"That'll be us one day." He winked at me adorably. There was a chorus of oohs and aahs, and some of the other players made obnoxiously embarrassing kissing noises. Honestly, the teasing didn't bother me a bit. I was falling in love with Andy, simple as that.

As though reading my mind, Sydney leaned in close, whispering, "He's definitely the one for you." Even though Sydney was only an alternate, Coach Davis had asked her to come to this meeting today. Admiringly, she had recovered completely from the incident, at least physically. Genevieve was in attendance tonight too. She'd recuperated from her poisoning just fine, and was as bitchy as ever. Unsurprisingly, she and Ronnie had mended ways, and were officially dating again. I'd finally accepted the fact—they were a match made in heaven.

"Okay, girls…" Coach Davis said, pulling herself away from her fiancé and walking over to where we were sitting. "I have good news and bad news. The bad news is that I got a call from Principal Barlow last night. Apparently, she read something in Brittani's diary that she didn't like. It had something to do with dropping someone in a lift on purpose…" she said, looking at me slyly. *Coach Davis must have known all along when she saw Teresa fall!* I realized. I couldn't believe it! But then again, Coach Davis was very bright, so I sort of did.

"Anyway. Principal Barlow has decided to remove Brittani from the team due to these actions." We all gasped. I couldn't help smiling. It was somewhat ironic, really. Brittani bragged that, because of her mother, she would definitely be a cheerleader. As it turns out, being the principal's daughter worked against her in the long run. It reminded me of a saying I heard once—*karma's a bitch.*

"And the good news?" Tally asked skeptically.

"Meet your newest squad member." Coach Davis pointed to where Sydney was sitting, Indian style, on the floor in front of the bench. Sydney's face was glowing. Everyone congratulated her, and I gave her a big hug. She deserved this, especially after everything she'd been through.

"Oh my gosh…look who's coming into the gym!" someone from up in the bleachers yelled, catching everyone's attention. The stands were filled with whispers, and everyone was looking toward the doorway. My eyes darted to where they were pointing. It was Amanda's Grandma Mimi!

I had to admit, I was shocked to see her myself. I'd lived next door to the lady for as long as I remember, and I'd only seen her a handful of times. After nearly ten years of hiding in her house, Mimi Loxx had come to Harrow High to see her granddaughter cheer. She was walking slowly, with her head down, a heavy shawl draped around her despite the hot weather. Each of her fingers was covered in shiny jewels, and she was wearing a flashy, sequin-covered beret on her head. Despite her age, she still looked like a Vegas showgirl in her own right.

I was worried for a moment that Amanda might be embarrassed by her, but I was wrong. Amanda jumped to her feet. "That's my grandma!" she shouted proudly, running over to her grandmother's side.

Sydney and I looked at each other, sharing a smile. "Congrats on making the squad, Syd," I told her, and I meant it. My best friends were having a lucky night, and I was happy for them both.

I am pretty lucky myself, I realized, looking up in the stands at my mom, dad, and little brother. My dad had somehow managed to get the night off, and I was thrilled to have him there. It was moments like this when I realized what was really important in life. My family and friends were everything to me, and I never wanted to lose them.

So far, my freshman year of high school had been eventful, to say the least. Looking around the gym at some of my classmates, I couldn't help but wonder what would happen next in my lovely town of Harrow Hill…I'd heard a rumor around town that people had nicknamed my school "Horror High" after the incident with Ashleigh. I sincerely hoped that wasn't true.

The game was getting ready to begin. As I was reaching for my pompoms, I noticed my iPhone flashing. I glanced at it quickly, seeing a missed call from an unknown number. I was suddenly reminded of Ashleigh's creepy phone call that night weeks ago, when she threatened that I would die if I went to a game.

Suddenly, my phone chimed again, alerting me that I had a voicemail. With only a minute to go before the game started, I lifted the phone up to my ear to listen. Horrifyingly, I recognized the creepy, robotic voice instantly. *But it can't be Ashleigh, because she's locked away in jail awaiting trial*! I thought frantically.

The voice said: "I warned you not to go to the games, Dakota. You should have listened. Now you're going to die…"

Epilogue

The Sociopath

Today is the day…for celebrating, that is…

I can't believe that idiot Ashleigh actually followed through with my orders. I might be even smarter than I initially thought. Now that she's locked away, I'm going to lay low…biding my time, toying with my prey. This is more fun than just blowing them away with my gun.

When the time is right, I'll kill them all. One student at a time.

The cheerleaders are first on my list.

Acknowledgements

Thank you to my mother, who attended every single game and rooted for me at every stage of my life.

Thank you to Flocksdale's Finest street team and all of my fans for your love and support!

Thank you to Jennifer O'Neill and Jessica Gunhammer for letting me share my stories with the world. I feel grateful to be a part of Team Limitless.

Thank you to Lori Whitwam for your help, guidance, and support at every step of the process.

Thank you to my amazing editor, Toni Rakestraw. I don't know what I'd do without your help.

Thank you to Ashley Byland of Redbird Designs for my beautiful cover art. You always nail it and I appreciate all of your hard work.

Thank you to Elise Balt for your daily help with all of the small and big things.

Thank you to Dixie Matthews for formatting my books and being so kind and helpful.

Thank you to Lydia and Crystal for all of your help with promotions.

Thank you to Mitsy Princell for helping me organize events and for being an awesome friend and fan.

Thank you to Mia of happianarky.com for designing promos for me and setting up my website.

Thank you to all of my beta-readers; your feedback is invaluable to me and I can't thank you enough.

So many people to thank! Thanks to all my

family and friends, and all of the other staff at Limitless Publishing for your incredible support along the way.

About the Author

Besides my family, my greatest love in life is books. Reading them, writing them, holding them, smelling them…well, you get the idea. I've always loved to read, and some of my earliest childhood memories are me, tucked away in my room, lost in a good book. I received a five dollar allowance each week, and I always—always—spent it on books. My love affair with writing started early, but it mostly involved journaling and writing silly poems. Several years ago, I didn't have a book to read so I decided on a whim to write my own story, something I'd like to read. It turned out to be harder than I thought, but from that point on I was hooked. I'm the author of *The Flocksdale Files Trilogy*, *This Is Not About Love* and *Grayson's Ridge*. I'm a total genre-hopper. Basically, I like to write what I like to read: a little bit of everything! I reside in Floyds Knobs, Indiana with my husband, three children, and massive collection of books. I have a degree in psychology and worked as a counselor.

Facebook:
https://www.facebook.com/CarissaAnnLynchauthor

Twitter:
https://twitter.com/carissaannlynch

Blog:
https://carissaannlynch.wordpress.com/

Goodreads:
https://www.goodreads.com/author/show/11204582.Carissa_Lynch

Website:
http://carissaannlynch.com/

39110436R00140

Made in the USA
San Bernardino, CA
19 September 2016